THE RISE OF
LUBCHENKO

THE RISE OF
LUBCHENKO

Michael Simmons

razOr
bill

The Rise of Lubchenko

RAZORBILL

Published by the Penguin Group
Penguin Young Readers Group
345 Hudson Street, New York, New York 10014, U.S.A.
Penguin Group (USA) Inc., 375 Hudson Street, New York, New York 10014, U.S.A.
Penguin Group (Canada), 90 Eglinton Avenue, Suite 700, Toronto,
Ontario, Canada M4P 2Y3 (a division of Pearson Penguin Canada Inc.)
Penguin Books Ltd, 80 Strand, London WC2R 0RL, England
Penguin Ireland, 25 St Stephen's Green, Dublin 2, Ireland
(a division of Penguin Books Ltd)
Penguin Group (Australia), 250 Camberwell Road, Camberwell,
Victoria 3124, Australia (a division of Pearson Australia Group Pty Ltd)
Penguin Books India Pvt Ltd, 11 Community Centre, Panchsheel Park,
New Delhi - 110 017, India
Penguin Group (NZ), Cnr Airborne and Rosedale Roads, Albany,
Auckland 1310, New Zealand (a division of Pearson New Zealand Ltd)
Penguin Books (South Africa) (Pty) Ltd, 24 Sturdee Avenue, Rosebank,
Johannesburg 2196, South Africa

Penguin Books Ltd, Registered Offices: 80 Strand, London WC2R 0RL, England

10 9 8 7 6 5 4 3 2 1

Library of Congress Cataloging-in-Publication Data is available

Printed in the United States of America

for Gordon and Tatum

ACKNOWLEDGEMENTS

The author wishes to thank Thaddeus Bower, Anne Dahlie, Elizabeth Dahlie, Susan Dahlie, Eloise Flood, Kathrin Kollman, Allison Lynn, George Nicholson, and Paul Rodeen.

H alfway through the second semester of my junior year, I saw exactly one man get killed. Shot in the back when he didn't expect it. But he was a bad guy. Really bad. By almost anyone's standards, he had it coming. My father's business partner did it. Mr. Richmond. He put a bullet in the bad guy's head and saved my life. Brought an end to a pretty strange time for me. But only for a while. Looking back, I'd say that when Mr. Richmond saved me that night, it was really only the opening moments of something much, much stranger. But it's kind of a long story. Need to offer up a little background first.

S eeing that I'm fairly impatient (and I've documented all this before), I'd like to do this as quickly as possible. Here's a straightforward, no-frills recap of what you need to know. And if it's confusing, it's only because I myself am a very confused young man. This, at least, is what I'm told.

A Brief Word About Me

I am unnaturally handsome, extremely clever (although a surprisingly poor student), quite funny when harassing my father and my hostile teachers, and extremely greedy when it comes to matters of food and money. I'm a delight to be around. A friend to those in need. And women tend to find me highly attractive (or so I have no choice but to believe).

The First Crime

A guy named Belachek was found murdered one day in my father's office building. Quite a surprise. And devastating for my father since Belachek was a friend. Equally devastating was the fact that the cops accused my dad of the murder. And they accused him of a bunch of other things too, including the not-insignificant crime of bioterrorism. Outrageous. My father was the most law-abiding man in America. But there was evidence. Good evidence. This is because my dad was framed.

The Catch

For purposes that would be very clear if you met my dad, I used to steal office equipment from his medical company and sell it online. Pretty stupid, but I needed the money because my cheap-ass millionaire father never gave me any. Anyway, in the course of my theft operations, I accidentally stole Belachek's (the dead man's) computer, which happened to have evidence on it that could clear my father. For reasons that only my computer geek best friend understood, however, if I turned the computer over to the cops, I'd get busted for my criminal activities. So here was the catch: I could sit on the computer and watch my dad rot in jail, or turn the computer over to spring my father and go to jail myself. Very tricky, especially since my dad spent so much of his time tormenting me. In other words, why the hell should I help him?

My Unbelievable Heroism

Unable to accept the fact that my father was falsely imprisoned, and too cowardly to come clean to the cops, I flew to France with my two best friends. While there, I met with an international freedom fighter named Lubchenko (important for you to remember), tracked down the bad guys that framed my dad, foiled the shocking plans to sell smallpox virus on the black market (the smallpox virus has the potential to be an extremely dangerous biological weapon), and also (since we're discussing my achievements) convinced a girl to fall in love with me. Not bad, especially for a guy who's considered such a dope by all adult authority figures.

Mr. Richmond Saves the Day

Like I said, Mr. Richmond, my dad's business partner, shot a guy in the back of the head. This guy (one Mr. Rick Colburn) was about to shoot me and my friend Ruben right after we got back from France. Colburn was quite upset with me and Ruben because we had ruined his plans for world domination. But before Colburn could shoot, Mr. Richmond showed up and killed him. It was a little fishy to the cops. They get a bit nervous when there's lots of gunfire and mayhem. But Mr. Richmond had good lawyers. And he had a good excuse. He was just coming by to check on me while my dad was in jail. He carried a gun. He had a license. And he saw a guy about to kill a couple of teenagers. So he opened fire. Made sense. It all added up. But I should say this: during my escapades in Seattle and France, when I was fighting crime, I had reason to believe that Mr. Richmond was in on the whole bioterrorism thing. I had no solid proof. But I had plenty of reason to believe it. And if this was true, Mr. Richmond had killed the one guy who could finger him—that is, he killed Colburn. *This is important for you to know.*

S o this is where my story begins.

On a bright, cheerful summer's day (a Sunday, in fact), my dad walked into the kitchen, told me that he had to leave town that afternoon—for two weeks—and then reached into his pocket, pulled out five hundred dollars, and handed me the cash.

"That should take care of anything you need while I'm gone," he said. "Mrs. Andropolis will look in on you from time to time. She'll spend the night when she can."

Then my dad said he had to pack. "I'm leaving in an hour," he added, and disappeared up the back stairs.

Maybe for most people this kind of thing would not be so surprising. I don't know. I've only ever lived with my father. My sense is that it would probably be a little surprising. But the fact that my father acted this way was absolutely mind-blowing. Entirely incomprehensible. My father was a total hard-ass, a complete grouch, and (for extremely good reasons) didn't trust me one bit. Not at all. He was also as cheap as they come—as cheap as a man can be who's also a millionaire. He'd never slipped me so much as a twenty, and now he forked over five hundred bucks.

I looked at the money as I continued to scoop cereal into my mouth. I thought I should ask my father if everything was all right. Maybe he had some kind of sudden brain disorder. Maybe I had to get him to the hospital immediately. But then I thought, *My dad's splitting for two weeks and he just gave me a fistful of cash.* I decided not to push my luck. He might change his mind. When a man who's spent his life pushing you around suddenly gives you a wad of fifties and tells you he's leaving you alone, I say run with it. That's always been a kind of rule I've lived by. A personal code.

Now, I should say for the sake of the larger story (and perhaps you already know this) that my dad pretty much raised me. My mother died when I was young and left my father the impossible task of taking care of a very unruly boy. Pretty tough. That's no excuse for him doing as bad a job as he did. Still, a tall order, especially for a guy like my dad.

For my part, I spent most of my conscious life trying to humiliate, scandalize, and disgrace my father. This is what he always told me, at least.

"You're a complete disgrace," he liked to say. "You've completely disgraced me. There's simply no explanation of how you're my son."

Cruel, but true. Can't deny it. And in response to my delinquent (though charming and absolutely hilarious) behavior, my dad kept me on an extremely tight leash. The tightest in Seattle, by my estimation. No money. Early curfew. No car privileges. Strict private school for boys. Etc., etc., etc.

And this is why I was kind of worried that morning. And the

truth is that this wasn't the first time he had acted like this in recent weeks. He had given me money on other occasions. For no reason. Incredible. He didn't yell at me as much for missing curfew. And he only broke two lamps when he was screaming at me after I failed most of my classes that semester and ended up in summer school. If a UFO had landed on our front lawn, I would have been less amazed.

And there had been even stranger, more emotional events. He told me he was "glad I was around," for instance. I almost vomited. So did he. He only barely choked out the words. Seemed like he felt a kind of obligation to say it. And to counteract any sentimentality, he grounded me later that day when I accidentally scratched his car with a broken bottle I had found.

"What are you doing playing around with broken glass?" he screamed as he looked at the enormous scratch on the side of the car. "I mean, can you please tell me why you do this kind of thing? What reason could you possibly have to drag a broken bottle along the side of my car?"

It was a good question. Still, I'm a free spirit. An independent-minded young man. Sometimes I do things for no reason at all. I just said, "I thought you said you were glad I was around this morning."

"You're grounded," he screamed. "And if you ever bring that up again, I'll make you stay in for the whole summer." Then he stormed off. Some kind of gladness. Obviously I hadn't been missing very much. Still good to see the old man back to normal.

So, all very strange. Anyway, back to that morning. About an hour after telling me he was leaving, a taxi pulled up in front of our house and my dad lumbered downstairs with his suitcase.

I stood up to see him to the door. I wanted to watch him get into the taxi to make sure this wasn't some kind of trap. (My father was not above hiding in the bushes for the afternoon to see if I threw a party.)

My father looked over at me as he opened the front door and said, "Well, I'm off."

Then he looked a little more seriously at me—like he was going to start yelling. But all he said was, "Call Mrs. Andropolis to see when she's coming over."

And then (unexplainably) he put down his suitcase, reached into his pocket, and pulled out another two hundred bucks. "In case I get delayed coming back."

Again, shocking behavior. Frankly, it was one of the most spooky things that's ever happened to me. And I've had a gun pointed at my head.

"Where are you going?" I finally said. Seemed like he was never coming back—all this last minute generosity seemed to suggest that he was making some sort of peace with his creator before drifting off to the great beyond.

My dad hesitated. Finally he said, "I'm going to Brussels. Some unexpected business."

And then he picked up the suitcase again and walked down the path to the waiting taxi.

S o *Brussels* is code. Or it means something. If my dad was going to San Antonio or Tallahassee, I'd assume that he was going to some boring medical conference that I absolutely didn't want to know about. But Brussels is where NATO headquarters is—pretty much the biggest, most powerful military alliance the world has ever seen—and my dad's business there was always pretty freaky.

Again, my father's company (MRI, which he started and owned with Mr. Richmond) made medicine. High-end stuff that could cure people of some pretty nasty things. And in this vein, they also produced smallpox vaccine and sold it to friendly governments all around the world.

Why would anyone want to buy smallpox vaccine? Well, smallpox is a highly contagious, extremely deadly disease. And pretty frightening—bursts open all the cells in your organs for an absolutely agonizing death. Most relevant: it's long been considered the biological weapon of choice for terrorists. So, governments buy the vaccine with the idea that if some bad guys start to spread smallpox, they can inoculate their citizens. In fact, this is really the only use for the vaccine since smallpox hasn't occurred naturally since the 1970s. Anyway, MRI was one of the biggest vaccine producers in the world, and they sold lots and lots of it.

One more important point. To manufacture vaccines, you need access to live strains of the virus. That is, you need living samples of the very thing that world governments fear the most. MRI had this. They were what's known as a "hot lab." So, high-end, dangerous stuff. Lots of security. Lots of risk.

The final relevant point: smallpox had been kind of on my mind in those days. Like I said, I led a small squad of fearless teenagers into the jaws of hell to prevent an international conspiracy to sell live strains of smallpox—strains that came from my father's company, no less.

It had also seemed to come up other times. For instance, just after school got out for the summer, my father and I had the following fight. It was Friday morning, and there was suddenly banging on my door. It was early in the morning, like not even eleven, and I was still fast asleep.

"Get up, Evan," my father yelled.

"No," I replied.

My bedroom door flew open. "Get up! Now! I've something I need you to do."

"What?"

Normally I didn't have to do too many so-called chores because my father (quite rightly) didn't trust me with anything more than taking out the garbage. And I usually even messed that up.

"I want you to come down to MRI to get a smallpox vaccination. I want to make sure that everyone feels it's safe. I'm making it mandatory that everyone at MRI has one since we deal with the virus. And I don't want to look like I'm asking my staff to do something I won't ask my family to do."

"What if it's not safe?" I said. "What are they afraid of?"

"It's safe. A tiny percentage of people suffer side effects. But it's safe. You're young. You'll have no problems."

I should point out here that, at this particular time, I didn't want to get a shot. I'm not a big fan of pain.

"Why don't you get one?" I finally said, the covers still over my head.

"I've already had one. Anyway, now you have to get one."

"Why?"

"Because I said so," my dad yelled. I felt his beefy fingers clamping down around the back of my neck. It seemed that I wasn't going to have much choice in this matter. Great. Just what every sixteen-year-old wants to do on one of his first free mornings of the summer: get a smallpox shot.

Anyway, he marched me down to MRI, where all these people were lined up. Then he pushed me to the front of the line, pulled up my sleeve, and in the next second the company nurse was jamming a long, cold needle in my arm.

And then, afterward, sitting in a small room, I was asked to sign the legal release papers.

"Shouldn't I have seen all this before the shot?" I said, looking over the list of unlikely but possible side effects, including things like withering leg muscles, bleeding from the eyeballs, and "brain fever."

"Just sign it and stop being such a baby," my father said. So I did. What did it matter at that point? And that was that. When you think about it, I was actually a very obedient son. Most kids wouldn't have been so compliant. What a good son I was. Actually, more like my dad was a tough guy. Knew just how to put the pressure on if he had to.

Whatever. All background. And at the time, I didn't really put everything together. It was fairly weird that I had to get vaccinated like that. It was weird that the whole company was being vaccinated. But I didn't add it all up. Looking back at the whole thing now, however, I'd have to say it was all pretty important. It was all pretty relevant to the story I'm telling now.

S o I'd seen some pretty heavy crap for a guy **5**
my age. But I clung desperately to my
youthful idiocy as much as I could. You'd think
that nearly dying like I had would change my atti-
tude—make me shape up, as they say. But, as
usual, life's lessons were wasted on me, and I
learned absolutely nothing. My dad left. I thought
for a few minutes about the implications of my dad's nervous-
ness, and smallpox, and his rushing off to see his NATO con-
tacts in Brussels, and then I thought, *I've got to have a party.*
Seemed reasonable. It was summer.

First, I called Mrs. Andropolis, the woman who (as you may
know) kind of looked after my dad and me. It was a quick conversation. She was watching TV and didn't really want to talk.
She said she'd stay the night whenever I wanted.

"You tell me what you want," she said. "You don't need me
to tell you what to do. You just tell me what you want."

What a woman. Mrs. Andropolis trusted me implicitly, and
showered me with love. A mistake, maybe, in the eyes of some.
But the truth is she was the only adult on the planet who could
make me feel guilty about anything. And after I told her I didn't
need her to come over that night, I even felt a little bad. Like,

was I taking advantage of her? But Mrs. Andropolis was always encouraging me to have a good time. And she was always covering for me when I was in trouble. And she was always pissed off at my father for being so hard on me. So it seemed like having a big party was a good idea. I told Mrs. Andropolis I was fine for the weekend, thanked her for treating me like a capable and responsible young man, then hung up and began to plan for the night.

First, a call to Ruben.

"Ruben," I yelled into the phone.

"I'm busy," he quickly replied. "Whatever it is, I can't do it."

"You don't even know what I'm going to say."

"I can tell by the tone in your voice that I'm not interested."

"Ruben, my dad's gone. For two weeks. Come over. I'm having a party."

There was now a pause. I was sure Ruben wanted to come over at this point, but he didn't want to look weak or like he'd let me talk him into anything. But he wanted to come over. He definitely wanted to come over.

"Ruben?" I said again.

"I'll be right over," he finally replied.

Nothing like an unsupervised house to impress your friends.

So it was early afternoon, and Ruben and I had the whole day ahead of us to do nothing but lounge around. I mean, this is what I would have done anyway: nothing. But doing nothing is always better when there are no angry parents around to disapprove. In fact, doing nothing when my dad was around was a lot of work. Psychological work. I was involved in an intricate game of disobedience and self-expression. When he wasn't there, I lounged around simply because I enjoyed it.

So, we watched a baseball game, made strawberry daiquiris, played soccer in the living room, goofed off in my dad's den— my father, predictably, had an excellent weapon collection— and did a million other pointless things, all sweetened by the fact that there was no angry man storming around complaining about my grades in algebra or my inability to conjugate so much as a single Latin verb—and I'd been taking Latin for a couple of years. (It actually takes a lot of effort to learn absolutely nothing over a span of two years.)

We also made a few calls—to set up the party. As is well known among our nation's youth, to throw a party, you only need to make one or two calls. Much more sophisticated than all the formal invitation crap of the parental sphere. Just one or two calls and everyone knows.

I also called my so-called girlfriend, Erika, and left a message. She was out, and I had no idea where. I'll get to her in a second, but she was torturing me at that particular moment in our relationship. I am what women call "desperately needy," which is not a quality most people find attractive in a mate. But again, I'll get to that. Have another important point to make at this juncture.

So Ruben and I were playing an improvised game of Ping-Pong on the dining room table (with a row of Austrian crystal wineglasses for the net) when there was a knock at the door.

I kind of freaked out at first—early party guests?

I wasn't ready.

Hadn't even picked out my outfit for the evening.

And then there was my hair to attend to.

But then I looked out the front window, and there was Mr. Richmond, my dad's business partner. Not a guest. That was good. But not good that it was Mr. Richmond. Kind of wigged me out, frankly. Here's why: strange as it may seem, ever since he saved my life, the guy really kind of creeped me out. There were a lot of unanswered questions. After all, I had once thought that Richmond was in on the whole bioterrorism thing. Second, and again, the guy who he killed (the guy who had been about to kill me) was the one dude who could have fingered Mr. Richmond, if he was in fact involved. So, he saved my life. But he had a lot to gain by doing it. Whatever.

And more generally, besides the whole bioterror-killer thing, I'd always found Mr. Richmond a bit slimy. Strange, because he was a highly accomplished human being and profoundly smart. No joke. Fancy medical degree, significant research achievements, and a great businessman. But he always seemed to be trying to be something that he wasn't. Slick, cool, flashy, etc. And frankly, that's almost as bad as being an international killer.

Still, I opened the door. No matter how much a guy freaks you out, you have to open the door when he knocks.

"What's up, Evan?" he said as I opened the door. "Was just

passing by and thought I'd check in on you. Planning a little fun while the old man's away?"

"I guess so," I replied. Again, it was always a tough negotiation. Mr. Richmond was always trying to be my "pal," but who wants to confess to an adult that you're having a party?

"That's what I'd do," he said. "In fact, that's what I *am* doing while your dad's away. I'm planning on goofing around myself. Might not go into work Monday."

"You're traveling next week too, right?" I said. (This is what I had heard.)

"Going to Switzerland to look at ski chalets. I want one, but it will also be good for business. A great place to bring clients. And the Swiss medical companies are booming. I'm trying to set up a couple partnerships with them. I'll be in lots of meetings. But I'll be having fun too. Not the kind of thing your dad could do. All that relaxing and having a good time makes him pretty nervous."

I laughed as he said this, but (again) I have to say that if anything made my dad's stingy, boring outlook seem reasonable, it was Mr. Richmond. I desperately wanted to drive around in a high-end German sports cars like him. But Mr. Richmond made the whole thing seem a little gross. Kind of like having the opportunity to eat a whole chocolate cake in one sitting: the idea seems great, but when you do it, you feel kind of sick. (And I've done it.) (Twice.)

Anyway, Mr. Richmond stepped into the front hall and we

talked about this and that. He knew Ruben (had actually saved his life as well because the freak killer Colburn was going to shoot us both). They shook hands and said hi, and Mr. Richmond asked, "How's it going, big guy?"

And then Mr. Richmond said he had to leave. "Do you need anything?" he asked. "I'm around if you do." He paused. "Beer? You want me to buy you beer?"

I assured him that we didn't need beer, although this was an appealing offer. Still, there were eight million people with fake IDs that would be bringing beer that night, and I thought it was best to decline. If Mr. Richmond bought me beer, I'd never hear the end of it. "How was that beer, big guy?" he'd say every time I saw him.

"We're fine," I said, and then added, for the sake of plausibility, "We've always got my dad's liquor cabinet."

Mr. Richmond laughed. "Now you're talking," he said. And then he put up his hand, waved it in the air, turned, and headed out the door. "Give me a call if you need anything."

And that was it. There he went. Mr. Richmond.

S o, enter romantic interest.

About half an hour later, as Ruben and I were still playing Ping-Pong and enjoying our delicious frozen daiquiris, Erika stopped by. Again, there was an unexpected knock on the door. But this time, looking out the window produced a much better result.

"Got your message," she said as soon as I opened the door. "Good news, huh? Dad's gone for a couple of weeks." She stepped forward and kissed me politely on the cheek. Erika liked me. Really. I'd say we had a good relationship. But I need a lot of attention. A lot. I'm very troublesome to a girlfriend, especially if she has any kind of independent spirit. But Erika liked me. She just had to keep me under control.

For instance, here's a sample of the kind of phone conversation we often had:

Me: Can I come over?

Erika: I'm in the middle of something, Evan.

Me: Please?

Erika: I'm doing something.

Me: Come on. What are you doing?

Erika: I'm studying.

Me: Studying what?

Erika: Math.

Me: Can I come over?

Erika: No.

Me: Please?

Erika: No.

Me: What are you doing?

Erika: I'm studying, Evan. My God.

Me: Can I come over?

Erika: No.

Me: Please.

Erika: No.

As you can see, it was an enormous act of generosity that Erika even spoke to me. And I should really point out that she could have done much better. She was a tall, chiseled, entirely symmetrical woman—the type so idealized by our crass popular American culture. Frankly, I'm not interested in that kind of woman at all. Not at all. But I was interested in Erika, so what could I do? Had to go out with her.

Whatever. She walked in, poked Ruben in the chest and told him he was eating too many doughnuts, and then walked into the back hall and toward the kitchen.

"Game over," I said, putting down my Ping-Pong paddle.

"But I'm winning," Ruben yelled.

"Ruben, I have to attend to my girlfriend."

"I'm not sure how much more of this relationship I can take," he replied. He stood there for a moment, then dropped his paddle in disgust and followed me back to the kitchen.

Anyway, not much more to say about the rest of the afternoon. It was all spent in happy anticipation of the evening ahead, which is the very best way you can spend an afternoon. Really enjoyable. Playing music, defrosting frozen pizzas, watching TV, and just generally goofing around. It was really great. Sadly, though, as often seems to happen with me, my good times were spoiled by a fairly unexpected (and extremely serious) distraction.

So, I've distilled all I've learned over the years into a small but potent maxim. Here it is (I suggest you memorize it):

Keep your mouth shut,
don't take things that don't belong to you,
don't mess around with things you don't know
about.

Follow this advice, and you'll live to a hundred. Fail to follow these simple rules, and it's not unlikely that a strange man in a dark overcoat will put a knife to your neck and teach you the last lesson you'll ever learn.

As for me, although I am, in fact, the maxim's author, I have never learned it.

Anyway, here's how phase two of my strange adventure began.

It was early evening. I was sitting in the kitchen with Ruben and Erika, eating an enormous banana and thinking that this was really one of the biggest bananas that I'd ever seen, let alone eaten. It was shocking, and I was thinking about how big a monkey would have to be to fit it into its mouth. Big, I concluded.

And then I started wondering if monkey mouths were bigger than human mouths and was fairly surprised that I had never asked this question before.

And then the phone rang.

I wasn't sure if I should answer it or not. I didn't want to lose hold of these brilliant thoughts. But I was having a party, and things were gearing up, so, very reluctantly, I got out of my chair and answered the phone.

"Hello?" I said.

"Evan Macalister?" the voice replied.

"Speaking."

"I've got some news that might interest you."

"Okay," I said. I momentarily wanted to make some kind of glib, funny comment. But the voice sounded older and very somber—not some teenager telling me he was bringing twenty of his best friends over to my house.

"I'm going to keep this simple because I know you know what I'm talking about. Tomorrow morning, Jim Richmond will personally be transporting live strains of the smallpox virus to Switzerland, where he'll be selling the virus to black market arms dealers. After that, he's going to kill your father in Brussels. And then he's going to kill you and your friends."

Needless to say, I was fairly dumbstruck. A million questions buzzed through my head, but by the time I opened my mouth to speak, the guy had hung up.

"Hello?" I said. "Hello?"

Useless. No one was there.

Finally I hung up the phone and looked over at Ruben and Erika—they were both fooling around with their daiquiri straws.

After a moment or two, Erika looked up at me and said, "Who was that?"

"I don't know," I replied. "But he didn't have very good news for us."

"Great," Ruben said. He had a smirk on his face, like I was just up to my old charming high jinks. But he wasn't going to like this.

W hat?" Ruben yelled. "He said what?"

"We're all going to be killed," I replied. "He said Mr. Richmond is going to kill all of us." (Ruben always brought out the calm, thinking-man act in me.)

"Great, Evan. Great. We're all going to be killed. Well, that's cool. We'll all be killed. I guess it's got to happen sometime. Don't you think this is a little bit alarming?"

"And he's going to sell the smallpox virus to terrorists," I added. "Don't forget that."

"Awesome. World destruction. So what do you think we should do, smart guy?"

"Well, let's not panic," I replied. "We'll come up with something."

"Yeah. We'll come up with something." Ruben was now using very sarcastic tones. (Very offensive, really. Not at all helpful.) "I almost got my head blown off a couple of months ago," he continued. "I'm not doing that again. Let me tell you what we're going to do. Here's the plan. We're calling the cops. And I'm not discussing this any further."

I wanted to reply, but I had to admit that it also occurred to me that this was probably the best option. Still, we did have to discuss it. Couldn't do anything rash. Remember, the whole reason we ever got involved in all this was to cover my tracks (and Ruben's) in our theft of office equipment from my father's company. So if we went to the cops in the wrong way, we could get in pretty big trouble.

"I'm calling right now," Ruben said, standing up and walking to the phone.

I quickly raced to him and intercepted him. Gently.

"You're right, Ruben. You're right," I said. "We'll call the cops. But we have to do it the right way. There's no reason to get ourselves into trouble unnecessarily. I agree that we can't handle this ourselves. But let's not start confessing our own criminal history."

"But we're calling," Ruben asked.

"We're calling. I promise. We'll definitely call. Let's just figure out how to do it."

"Okay. Okay. But first let's cancel the party," Ruben said, now slapping his face and trying to get himself to be a little more alert. "We've got to talk about this. I'm not going to have this discussion with a bunch of drunk football players wandering around. Especially if someone's going to be trying to kill us."

I looked at Erika. I didn't really want to cancel the party and thought she might be into going forward with it.

She just looked at me and said, "Get real, Evan. Cancel the party. We have a lot to talk about."

Anyway, I got on the phone and started to make calls.

L et me say for the record that there's almost nothing harder to do in the world than call off a party once the wheels are in motion. I mean, call one person to announce a party, and the whole city knows. Call to cancel, and people somehow can't understand what you're saying. So for the rest of the evening and night we had to chase people away. There was nothing we could do. Carload after carload of people just kept showing up, and I kept having to tell them to get lost.

And some people were pretty insistent. Like, some of the beefy sports types weren't all that psyched to take orders from a scrawny (yet highly handsome) guy like me. Erika fielded those guys. She was pretty good at getting her way where football players were concerned.

Other people were just too stupid to figure it out. We told one group of kids to get lost and ten minutes later they were back again, like they had never even been there.

"Are you having a party, dude?" the guy said.

"No," I replied. "No party. How many times do I have to tell you?"

"Dude, take it easy," he said. "We thought there was a party here. If there's no party, there's no party. You don't have to get all freaked out."

Still, the constant flow of people continued, and it kind of sucked. We had some pretty serious stuff to talk about, after all.

"I can't hear myself think," Ruben kept saying as we sat in the kitchen discussing our options.

Finally I suggested that we all head to my dad's small upstairs library. We could draw the curtains, put on a tiny reading lamp, and turn off all the other lights in the house.

"People will figure out that there's nothing going on," I said.

But amazingly, the no-lights thing didn't help very much. No one was able to figure anything out. It was times like this that I was inclined to agree with my father's opinion that "young people are all complete idiots." I mean, a completely dark house, and people still wouldn't give up.

One group, for instance, just kept pushing the doorbell for fifteen minutes. They wouldn't leave.

Finally I went down, screamed my head off, told them to get lost, and then put up a sign that said, NO PARTY.

And then, ten minutes later, another group showed up and started hammering on the doorbell again. For another fifteen minutes. Unbelievable.

"Didn't you read the sign?" I asked when I arrived back at the door.

"Yeah, we read the sign," they said.

"And?"

"We thought there was a party."

"But it says that there's NO PARTY."

"Yeah, but we thought there was one."

Totally insane.

But the very worst was this one group that just crawled in through an open window. No one answered the door, so they just let themselves in. I found them in the living room hanging out when I went down to the kitchen to grab some Cokes.

They were kind of a tough problem for me, though. They were all from Pencrest Academy—my strict all-boys school—and they didn't like me all that much. They were all recent grads, all muscle-bound high achievers on their way to college, and none of them was too interested in taking orders from the dopey younger guy, who really had no business even speaking to them.

Again, I turned this one over to Erika. These guys were all handsome types—all had a lot going for them. But they hadn't gone to high school around girls. And that's a major handicap. Erika just walked in and said, "Boys, I'd love to hang out with you. I really would. But we're kind of tied up with something and there's no party tonight. Could you please do me a favor and head out? I'll owe you. I mean it."

There was no arguing with that. What could these idiots say to such a nice request from a girl?

I was, however, a little upset with the "I'll owe you" business.

"What the hell does 'I'll owe you' mean?" I said. "You won't *owe* them."

"Calm down, Evan. It's just an expression."

"And that's the last time you'll be using it," I replied.

Erika turned and poked me in the chest. But she also smiled and kissed me on the cheek. Amazing how being needy and demanding can actually make a woman happy sometimes. But I must here put the stress on the word *sometimes*.

Anyway, despite all the mayhem, we did actually manage to discuss various aspects of our situation.

"It really creeps me out," Ruben said. "I don't like the idea of anyone knowing what we know about the smallpox strains and our whole trip to Paris."

"Well someone obviously does," I said. "I just don't know why he'd want to call us with the information."

"Maybe he doesn't want us to die," Ruben said. "That's a good reason for a tip-off. I mean, it's not like this doesn't affect us. We seem to be on Richmond's to-do list."

Again, grim. I kind of didn't even know what to say. But the fact is that there wasn't really all that much to discuss in the end. "Bottom line is that you're right, Ruben," I said. "We've got to tell the police. But I think we should make it anonymous as well. Our own anonymous tip. And then we'll be done with it. No need to tell anyone our story. We'll just say that Richmond is planning on smuggling smallpox out of the country."

"But will the cops believe us?" Ruben asked. "I mean, we're

not giving them much to go on if we call anonymously and just tell them what we heard."

It was kind of a good question. Cops must get a million crank calls a day. And we didn't have any evidence to speak of. Just an accusation, with no facts to back it up. Hard to believe that you can just call the cops and get someone in trouble without providing photographs and bank records and bloody fingerprints.

But in the end, this was very serious stuff. Cops couldn't ignore it. "They'll believe us," I said. "They'll have to. No choice. Can't take a tip like this lightly. Not in this day and age."

The other question that we were all asking ourselves was who exactly made the call. "I wonder who this guy is and why he called us," Erika said. "I mean, why didn't *he* just tip off the cops?"

"Maybe he's on the inside—can't get involved," I said.

"He called us," Erika replied.

"Maybe he couldn't tell the cops that Richmond was going to kill us as well—that kind of info would lead the cops to us, and maybe he doesn't want the cops to know about what went down this spring. He could have called us to help us out without having to get the police in on it."

There was a pause. Then Erika asked, "Did the guy have any kind of accent?"

"Totally neutral," I said. "Perfect English."

"Did you recognize the voice at all?" she asked. "Anything that seemed familiar?"

I thought hard for a moment, then said, "No, nothing."

"I wonder who it was," Erika said.

"Well, definitely someone somehow connected to Lubchenko and Richmond," I said. "Whether he's deep in their organizations or just a lackey on the fringes, I don't know. But not many people know about what happened to us this spring. It has to be someone connected to that somehow. Could be an ally of Lubchenko's. Could be an enemy of Richmond's. There are a lot of possibilities."

"Maybe it's just a prank," Ruben suddenly said. "Maybe someone's just playing a prank on us."

"Whoever made the call knows a lot of heavy stuff," I replied. "I don't think someone so down on the international crime circuit would bother to play a joke on three teenagers. Anyway, the bottom line is that a guy who's connected with bad dudes is calling us. That's as real as it gets. And we've seen enough to know what all this involves. Two guys died a couple of months ago. And Richmond killed one of them, as much as he claimed it was to save our lives. I don't think we can do anything but accept this caller as the real thing."

Erika and Ruben paused for a moment, then nodded in agreement. "This is real," Erika said.

So, this discussion went on for a while, but we really just kept repeating ourselves. In the end, there wasn't much more to say. There really was only one conclusion, one choice. Had to call the cops and tell them that something was going to go down with Richmond the next day.

So by about midnight, after talking it all over, we decided that we'd drive to a pay phone in one of the Seattle suburbs. That way we'd be harder to trace if, in fact, such a thing is even possible. They do it on TV. And that's enough evidence for me. But who knows? Anyway, we decided to make three calls—one to the general FBI hotline number we found on the Internet, one to the Seattle police hotline, and one to the airport security hotline. We figured it would register with at least one of them.

We also decided that Erika should make the call, because teenage girls rarely make crank calls to the police. This is well known. And we needed everything to be taken seriously.

"Why is it always me?" Erika complained as we left Seattle city limits.

"Always you? It's always me," Ruben replied.

"Ruben, you're the most gutless coward I've ever met," Erika said. "How could it always be you?"

"It's always me *because* I'm a coward. Evan likes to pick on me."

"That's true," I said. "I do like to make Ruben do things because he's such a coward. He's got you there."

Erika punched me on the arm.

Anyway, after driving a little more and arriving in a suburb called Bridgewater, we stopped in front of a boarded-up restaurant that had an old pay phone standing out front. It was a good phone because there was no one around and there was no real chance of anything like security cameras—just in case the call got traced. We also put on gloves for this reason—didn't want to leave prints.

We parked right in front of the phone, jumped out, huddled together by the phone, and started making calls, Erika doing the talking. We dialed *69 to eliminate caller ID and we kept the calls quick. This is what Erika said to all three hotlines: "I have some information you might be interested in. Tomorrow morning Mr. Jim Richmond, co-chairman of Macalister-Richmond Industries, will be boarding a plane for Switzerland carrying live strains of the smallpox virus. He plans to sell the virus to arms dealers. This is not a joke. This is for real. I'm calling other law enforcement agencies to make sure this message gets heard." And then she quickly hung up.

She made this call three times, and then that was it. Would have been nice to have details like flight information. But cops would figure that out with a quick computer search. Seemed like this message would do the trick, although we all kind of sweated it for the rest of the night and into the next day—the day that Mr. Richmond was scheduled to leave.

So I should say that one of the obstacles in my life at that moment was that I was enrolled in a so-called summer enrichment program. Basically, it was summer school at my high-end, uptight private school. The thing I hated about the title is that it sounded voluntary. Like I'd show up because I felt like "becoming enriched." Of course, unexplainably, this was true for some people. To each his own, I guess. Whatever you want. But me, I was forced into it with the following ultimatum: attend summer enrichment or repeat your junior year. It was an easy decision. An extra year at Pencrest was out of the question. I'd live with being there over the summer.

I'd actually done pretty well over the years not to fail more classes. I was actually quite good at doing the "bare minimum." In fact, I have an uncanny ability to find out what the bare minimum is in any situation and do exactly that. But the previous semester was a bit different. Yes, flying to France, saving the world, and almost dying was slightly troubling. But it wasn't from any kind of psychological trauma that I failed all my classes. It was more like too much celebration. I figured, *Given all I've accomplished, how could I possibly go back to studying algebra?*

But this is an interesting problem about life. No matter how thrilling things become, you've still got to do boring stuff half the time. Best to accept that right away, otherwise you'll end up in summer school.

Anyway, that Monday was the first day, and, as might be imagined, I had a hard time concentrating. I was really wondering what had happened with the calls and if, in fact, someone was going to shoot me later that afternoon. I had called Mrs. Andropolis to tell her to come over that day—for after school. Amazing that I could sink so low as to have an old woman around for my protection. But Mrs. Andropolis was tough. A tough cookie. If anyone could save me, it would be her.

But for all my wondering, when I finally made it home, my questions were answered pretty quickly. After saying hi to Mrs. Andropolis, I walked to the TV room and flipped on the local news, and there he was, Mr. Richmond, being led by FBI agents and airport security guards through the airport with a million television cameras following him. Extremely strange.

"That's your dad's business partner," Mrs. Andropolis said. "My God. I wonder what's happening. You know, I never trusted him. I wonder what he did."

And then, suddenly, I felt completely sick.

I didn't like the idea that my actions could have so much impact on the world. And let's face it: the only evidence I had against Mr. Richmond was a strange guy calling me up while I was eating a big banana. Not much to go on. But if you think about it, that's all the cops had as well, and they were clearly going crazy.

Anyway, the TV. There was just a lot of strange footage for a while: Mr. Richmond being led through an employees-only door at the airport, lots of fire trucks parked out front, the airport evacuated, etc., etc. And there were all these guys walking around in these yellow space suits—haz-mat suits, as they're called (*haz*ardous *mat*erial suits). So, all pretty serious.

But the cops were keeping their mouths shut. They held a press conference and said they had information that required emergency action. But they didn't say what it was.

That was the first press conference. Two hours later, they held another one, which I watched while drinking a very large milk shake that Mrs. Andropolis made for me (she was furious that I had to go to school in the summer and was working hard to ease my pain). Anyway, in the second press conference, they had more to say. The airport had (obviously) been evacuated, they had things under control, and now they made the announcement that I expected: they had received information that "a person of interest" was transporting hazardous biological materials to Switzerland. There was no mention of bioterrorism or Richmond specifically. But you didn't have to be a genius to figure it out, especially since the newscasters came on and it was all they could talk about.

As one announcer put it, "MRI was rocked with scandal and allegations of bioterrorism four months ago with the murder of

Emil Belachek. And now they seem to be up against the wall again. In particular, Jim Richmond appears to be the target of this investigation."

The police announcement was brief. They took no questions. It was just a guy in a blue hat saying the bare minimum before exiting behind a large metal door.

But Mr. Richmond's lawyer held a press conference moments after that. And he had a lot to say, especially since it was more than clear who the person of interest was. The lawyer said his client was being mistreated, slandered, and abused based on no evidence; that we lived in the United States, where a person is innocent until proven guilty; that the actions of the FBI and the Seattle police had gravely injured Mr. Richmond's reputation; and that as soon as his client was released, they would be pursuing "each and every course of action against the FBI and the city of Seattle."

To be honest, at this point, I was ready to jump in a car and head to Canada. I was suddenly freaking out that they were going to somehow trace the call and that I'd be spending my summer in juvie rather than summer school. Summer school actually seemed pretty good at that moment, and I took out my algebra book and began working very, very hard.

12

Anyway, for that day this was the main story on the news. Everyone was wondering if the rich medical exec was going down.

And the next morning, everyone had their answer.

Mr. Richmond was not going down.

He was totally clean.

They searched him, his bags, his house, his office, and they found nothing.

And Mr. Richmond's handlers were a little pissed off about it all.

In fact, just after Mr. Richmond was released from interrogation, the lawyer got in front of the cameras again and said he was going to sue the Seattle police and the FBI for numerous offenses and infractions.

"On absolutely no evidence, my client was led away in chains and deprived of his civil liberties for fourteen hours. Do we really live in a country where a man can be treated like this just because someone made a crank call? Think about it. Some kid calls up the FBI and a man's reputation is suddenly rocked to its foundations."

I was watching this before heading off to get my daily dose

of summer enrichment but decided I might be late, even if it was only my second day. I didn't like that reference to "some kid." Very alarming, in fact. I suddenly had this vision of me and Ruben and Erika being led away in front of TV cameras as some announcer described *"three sick teenagers playing a practical joke."*

A terrible image. But my focus quickly shifted. Suddenly Mr. Richmond stepped up to the microphone. I didn't want to hear it. But Mr. Richmond was like he always was—looking cool as a cucumber and flashing this very relaxed smile. In fact, he didn't look bothered at all. He nodded to the reporters, smiled again, then said, "I understand everyone was just doing their job. I'm not out to hurt the police or the FBI. I've done quite a bit over the years to support them, in fact. But it's important that private citizens not be put through what I've been put through. It's not just a violation of personal rights. This kind of wild-goose chase is a threat to national security. Our nation's defenses depend on a solid ability to process information, to separate fact from fiction. In this situation, I'm sorry to say that our institutions have failed us. I want to make sure that it doesn't happen again."

Then, from the pack of reporters standing in front of him, someone yelled, "What are you going to do now that you're out?"

Again, smiling and totally calm, he said, "I'm just anxious to put this behind me and get to Switzerland. I have clients waiting to meet me. And I'd like to do a little sightseeing."

There was another quick flurry of questions. But Mr. Richmond was done for the day. He paused for a moment, said, "Thank you," then stepped back and walked behind several bodyguards to a waiting black SUV.

There was another pause. And then the lawyer was back.

"My client is a kind man—a kinder man than I am—and I'm going to make sure that whoever is responsible answers for this harassment. And I'll tell you another thing—my client is going to Switzerland in the next day or so, and if they make him do anything more than pass through the metal detector, I'll bring the whole city government down."

And with that, the lawyer walked off to his own waiting black SUV.

Stunning.

I just sat there with my skin burning and feeling like I was about to die.

And then the phone rang.

"Evan?" (It was Erika.)

"Yeah."

"Did you see that?"

"I saw it."

"I hope this was the right thing to do. I mean, I hope we weren't wrong."

"I know, I know. But what choice did we have?"

"Just unbelievable what a scandal we caused."

"I wonder how the TV cameras got there so quick yesterday," I said. "Amazing that so much of this was recorded."

Then there was a pause—I think Erika and I were both mulling over the same thing. Finally I spoke up. "Either he's innocent or he's guilty. And if he's guilty, he's got it made. No way they'll check him like that again. He'll get through customs and security no problem. He could probably bring a bazooka on the plane at this point."

Erika hesitated, then said that it would be hard not to check him again. "He'll be on their list," she said. "They won't just let this drop, even if he's got an angry lawyer."

This was true, and I agreed. But the point was that they'd never scrutinize him as thoroughly again. If he was bringing the virus with him, he'd have it hidden, and there was no way they were going to go over him with the care they had the previous day. They couldn't. "And it's not that hard to hide this stuff," I said. "You can pack live virus in a sealed silicone container the size of a fingernail. Richmond could pack it any number of ways."

Another pause. And then Erika brought up another question: if he was transporting the virus, why was he clean? I mean, it was possible he was innocent. But it also seemed possible that he knew ahead of time, that he was tipped off somehow, in which case all this had really worked in his favor.

Erika and I were both silent for a moment. "Why don't you come over?" I finally said. "I'll call Ruben as well. We need to talk about this."

"I'll be right there," she said, and then she hung up.

Anyway, it was all a puzzle, and I was going over various courses of action in my head as I looked through the refrigerator for some kind of brain food when (now about a minute later) I got another call, somewhat related to this matter.

"Why the hell haven't you left for school yet?" the voice said. My dad. And he sounded pretty grouchy.

"Are you coming home for this?" I quickly asked. "I assume you've heard about Mr. Richmond."

My father sighed, then said, "I heard. But I'm not coming home. I'm working on something too important. And this airport crisis seems to have resolved itself. I hope."

I heard my dad sigh again, and then I proceeded to get a lecture about my study habits and how he shouldn't have to be calling me from Europe to make sure I got out of the house on time.

"I was just so surprised about Mr. Richmond," I said. "It's the kind of thing that can really distract a person."

"Get to school, Evan," my father replied. "Mr. Richmond's life doesn't concern you."

Anyway, we talked for another minute—my father gave me various further commands and instructions—and then we hung up. So much for that conversation.

I did think about what my father said about getting to school. But Erika was already coming over. And I had to talk to Ruben too. And let's face it, if I ignored the Richmond thing, there was a good chance I'd get shot. *I'm sure they'll under-stand at Pencrest,* I thought. *They'd want me to stay home.* This was not at all true. But I decided that this was the kind of situation where it's best *not to do* something and *say* you did. Kind of like lying, but in the interest of self-preservation and helping the world, which, as everyone knows, is always the best course of action. Always.

13

Anyway, the question was what to do. Richmond now had a free ride through international security, and it was likely that he was carrying smallpox with him. To top it off, his plans might well include killing me, which was something I preferred *not* to happen.

"We've got to do something," I said to Ruben and Erika as we sat by a large open window in my living room.

"We could call the cops again," Ruben said. "Tell them it was for real. We could tell them what happened in the spring—and that we already suspected Richmond was tied up in it."

"We'd still have no evidence. We have nothing but a very strange and unprovable story. Maybe it would get the cops excited if the airport incident hadn't just happened. But after yesterday and today, no one is going to give Mr. Richmond a hard time unless there's a photograph of him stuffing a million dollars down his pants."

There was a pause. And then I continued talking. "And I hate to bring this up, because I don't want to seem like I'm just covering my ass, but I don't want to start talking to the FBI and the cops about how we stole office equipment (and how we had the murdered man's computer and how we didn't come forward with this when my dad was rotting in jail) unless we can be pretty confident that this story is going to get us somewhere. I mean, I'll do it. If we have to. But I'm not going to do it if it won't get us anywhere."

I did feel guilty making this argument. I did feel like I was just covering my ass, despite what I said. But the fact was that it was true—fessing up to our criminal history wasn't going to get us anywhere.

There was another pause. Then Erika said, "Maybe that's why we got the anonymous call instead of the cops. The guy figured that it wouldn't do any good to tip off the cops directly. It obviously didn't work for us. Maybe we're supposed to do something ourselves. And let's face it: we're slated to die too. It seems pretty clear that we have to do something."

Another pause. We were racking our brains. And the pause continued. All very troubling. I did have an inkling of an idea. An inkling. But I couldn't quite get it out. It appeared, however, that I wasn't the only one thinking about it.

Finally, Ruben spoke up. "I wonder if we could track down Lubchenko."

Another pause. Then, "Kind of what I was thinking," I said.

Still, a difficult option. Was it possible? Would he help us? What would we even have to gain by this?

Anyway, with this troubling proposal on the table, let me quickly recap details about Lubchenko. Perhaps you already know them, but you'll at least need to keep them in mind going forward.

First Meeting

We met Lubchenko in the back of a café called the Saint-Beauvais in Paris last spring. It was Lubchenko's cryptic e-mails sent to the murdered man that led us to suspect Richmond's involvement in the murder of Emil Belachek—the murder that my dad was framed for. We used these e-mails to track Lubchenko down in Paris.

Lubchenko's Story

In the back room of the Café Saint-Beauvais, Lubchenko explained that he had helped to start a movement in his home-land (unnamed) that was fighting for its independence. This movement got out of hand and became more focused on making money than freeing anyone. They were acting as middlemen between bad guys at MRI (of which Richmond was probably one) and terrorist groups that were willing to pay millions for the smallpox virus. Lubchenko wanted to stop this. He was helping Belachek when Belachek was murdered. And when we found Lubchenko, he helped us as well.

What We Knew About Lubchenko

Nothing. Or, almost nothing. After he gave us evidence that would clear my father, we left with him telling us that he was leaving his backroom headquarters at the Café Saint-Beauvais. He didn't say where he was going or what he was doing. Lubchenko wasn't even his real name—he was just using it as a screen name when e-mailing with Belachek (the dead man). Still, it's the only name we knew, and it's what we called him.

A Small Detail

We did have one small piece of information about Lubchenko's real life. It was something he said in an offhand way the one time we met with him. He drove an old Mercedes and he got it fixed at a shop in a suburban town south of Paris called Champlan. The shop was called Lubchenko Auto. It was where Lubchenko took his alias from.

Anyway, back to the story.

"How will we find him?" Erika said.

This was a good question. But, as might be gathered from the *small detail* in the paragraph above, I kind of had an answer. It had actually occurred to me a long time ago—or last spring. It was a "just in case" kind of idea that I ended up not really needing at the time.

"We can go to Lubchenko Auto, in Champlan," I said, "and ask for a list of guys who drove old Mercedes."

Pause. Seemed plausible. Still, there was a little doubt.

"I don't think people like to give out information about their clients like that," Ruben said.

"They might tell us something. Three nice kids like us.

Maybe Erika can sweet-talk a mechanic into helping us out."

"I like how I'm always bait for you guys," she said. "You just use me to flirt our way to getting what we want. I think I'm a little offended."

"You should be flattered," I replied.

Anyway, we talked for a while, but that was the only plan we could come up with, if you could call it a plan. There were a few drawbacks.

First, there might be a lot of old Mercedes in a suburb of Paris. Still, we decided that there probably wouldn't be too many for us to check out.

Second, we didn't even know if any information from Lubchenko Auto would be at all helpful. It was likely that Lubchenko had split from France—he said he was breaking down the Café Saint-Beauvais, his headquarters. Maybe Lubchenko was somewhere in Moscow, planning to assassinate a public official. Or maybe he was wandering around Mexico City, hunting down old enemies. Still, we didn't have much to lose by trying.

Third, given Lubchenko's status as an international spymaster, he probably had some idea what was up already. Even if he didn't know beforehand, news of Richmond's arrest at the airport must have reached him by this point. He was actively involved with the terrorist organizations that were trying to get smallpox, even if he was secretly working against them. I mean, what did we have to add to the matter? But here's the deal:

Lubchenko might have already been working to stop the small-pox thing, but it might not have been on his mind to save our sorry asses. What did he care if we were killed? And this is why we had to do something. What if the sale was stopped, or inter-cepted, and Lubchenko left it at that? That still would leave a guy who wanted to blow my brains out. At the very least, we needed some help from Lubchenko to stop that from happen-ing. I mean, there's only so much a guy like me can do to defend himself, especially when he's up against another guy who's the linchpin in a bioterror scheme. Lubchenko, however, was probably the most intimidating man I'd ever met. Huge, strong, and a glare that froze you right in your tracks. Maybe the decision was less logical and more emotional—we just wanted a guy like Lubchenko on our side.

Finally, what the hell else were we going to do? The truth is that the only other idea I could come up with was to mix frozen drinks, watch some TV, and hope the world didn't end. Definitely my typical mode of operation, but it didn't seem very appropriate in this case.

And one more thing. We were scared. We really were. And at least tracking down Lubchenko would make us feel like we were doing something. So, blind and irrational fear. That was a reason to find Lubchenko.

Whatever. One thing was pretty clear. Had to head to France.

A s I've mentioned in the past at some length, **14**
we'd been to France before, so the ground-
work wasn't that difficult. We had passports, we
knew what customs and border control was like,
and we even knew where to get a good cocktail
at the Seattle airport. This time around, however,
we were faced with the small problem of cash. We
had *some*. My dad had left me that money. Erika and Ruben
had cash simply because they always did. And I even had a little stashed away from back when I stole office equipment from
my dad's company. But foreign travel can be quite expensive.
Quite costly. Especially since I tend to do expensive things. So I
devised a way to supplement our funds—the tried-and-true
method of stealing from my father. It always worked before,
although I want to state for the official record that this kind of
behavior is very, very wrong.

So one of the things about having millions of dollars is that
you tend to have nice things. Of course, most millionaires have
things like swimming pools and enormous TVs. This, sadly, was
not the case with my father. He went in for things like antiques
and art—"Timeless pieces that will never lose their value," as
he liked to say. For my money, I'd still prefer the swimming

pool. But the problem with the swimming pool is that it's not (as ironic as this sounds) a "liquid asset." That is, you can't exactly sell your swimming pool if you're looking for quick cash. But delicate silver pitchers, golden candlesticks, emerald-encrusted letter openers—they're the kinds of things you *can* sell. Now, if I wanted to get real money, I would have put such objets d'art up for auction at a fancy auction house. But we didn't exactly have time for that. And there's a lot of red tape. They kind of distrust teenagers who show up to sell that kind of thing. So I had to take what I got at a pawnshop (Tommy's Antiques and Collectibles), where the guy was definitely also suspicious of me, but was willing to look the other way because he was getting my father's things for so cheap.

"I need you to sign a few things," he said as he looked over a field general's sword from the Napoleonic Wars that I had taken from my father's den. "I've got to say, I don't often meet kids with this kind of stuff."

"I'm a unique young man," I said.

"And all this belonged to your mother?"

"To my mother. And when she died, it was all left to me."

Actually, it wasn't that implausible. My mother really had once owned half the stuff in the house, and if she had known what a stingy brute my father was going to be, I'm sure she would have willed everything she owned to me.

Anyway, the "few papers" this guy made me sign were more like "a million papers." He photocopied my driver's license a million times. I had to swear in the name of my government that the stuff belonged to me. And I think I even agreed to a provision that said they could cut out my tongue if I was lying. But if there's one thing I've learned over the years, it's to not pay too much attention to the details. If you do, you'll lose sight of the big picture. Words to live by, and the reason I'll sign almost anything put before me. There's always a way out. Anyway, I signed my name about thirty times—not exaggerating about that—and I walked out with just over $15,000 in cash, which, frankly, wasn't a third of what the stuff was worth. But it was only my father's stuff, so what did I care? Anyway, I was going to save his life, so what did he have to complain about?

Of course, I was probably going to get busted for all this. If my dad noticed the missing stuff (I mostly grabbed it from clos-ets and back rooms), I could always say we were robbed. True, if they ever traced the missing items, I had signed a lot of papers linking them to me. But what was I going to do? Had to be practical. There was a man out there selling deadly biologi-cal weapons—a man who wanted to kill me, no less. Had to take my chances. What good would the world be if my dad kept his stupid-ass things and I was dead? Think about it.

The other thing is that I had the option to buy the stuff back. If the trip came in under fifteen large, I could fork over the remainder of the money and repurchase some of my things for close to the same price I sold them for. That's how pawnshops work. Whatever. Not that big a concern, but if my dad ever went looking for his rare and beautiful sixteenth-century British sextant, he'd definitely blame me when he couldn't find it.

But I want to add one more thing. Generally relevant to all this. My dad also had a large safe in his den, the combination of which I had long ago stolen. There wasn't much useful stuff in there—just deeds to the house, life insurance policies, etc., etc., etc. But I checked it out when I was searching for stuff to hock and found stacks of gold bars and a large leather bag filled with gold coins. I grabbed a few of the coins—went toward the fifteen grand I got at Tommy's. But I had to be judicious. One of the bars was probably worth a fortune, but a missing gold bar would raise a lot more suspicion than an antique porcelain duck that sat on a side table in the living room. Anyway, the point is that this stockpiling of gold was kind of weird. Paralleled another new trend my father had, which was keeping hundreds of gallons of drinking water in the basement along with canned food, batteries, lots of flashlights, and even an enormous generator that he put in the garage (an enormous generator with lots and lots of gasoline). Call me paranoid, but I couldn't help but feel like my dad was extremely worried about some kind of disaster, and coupled with everything I knew and the absolutely unexplainable fact that my father had recently (and on more than one occasion) said he was happy to see me, that he was glad I was around, I'd have to say that my father's behavior was a little strange, a little alarming. Whatever. Just wanted to make the point.

And there were a couple of other travel details. Like explaining to the authorities that cared why I was skipping town. Summer school was simple. I wouldn't go. I mean, they didn't really expect me to go, did they? I didn't know how long we'd be away, but I figured I could deal with it. If it was a couple of days, I'd just do my time in detention and make a bunch of tearful apologies. If it was a matter of weeks, then I'd probably be dead anyway, so what did I care?

I did have to tell Mrs. Andropolis what I was up to, though. Pretty easy there as well. Erika, Ruben, and I just told the various adults in our lives that we were heading to the Oregon coast for a camping trip. Erika's and Ruben's parents were saints and they loved it when their kids did this kind of stuff. And Mrs. Andropolis loved it too.

"I'm so happy you're taking a little time off from all that hard work you do at school," she said. "They have no business making you go over the summer. I always thought that was a terrible idea."

She even said she'd call the school to tell them I was sick. "Lying is a virtue when done in the name of justice," she said. Who can say that's not true? Anyway, again, a remarkable woman. If only she had been my father. That would have been something.

I do have to say that I was a little nervous, though. Stealing from my father was one thing. But flunking summer school and having to repeat junior year would be a cosmic disaster—one on par with a worldwide smallpox epidemic. I figured I could handle it, however. I was a very resourceful (and unjustifiably confident) young man. *You'll land on your feet, you charming rascal,* I said to myself. *You always do.* Funny, even though not at all true.

And one other thing. A thing that was a bit more important. All this prep work was done immediately after the threatening phone call. So it was happening fast. But we wanted to know what Mr. Richmond's status was. That is, we needed to know if we were ahead of him. I thought about how to figure that one out but came up with a pretty simple plan. I'd call him up under the premise of getting him to buy us beer—he did offer—and just casually ask him.

So I called his office, and after two rings, I was talking to his secretary.

"Who is this, please?" the secretary said, after I asked if Mr. Richmond was in.

"This is Evan Macalister."

"Evan!" she screamed. "This is Cindy. Let me see if he's around."

It's common knowledge that power makes you attractive to women, and I'm pretty sure most of the secretaries at MRI had a crush on me because I was the boss's son. Of course, this is just speculation. I'm not exactly sure about this. But it seems like it might be true.

"Evan?" she said after a few moments.

"Yeah?"

"He's not in. Can *I* help you?"

"No. He just offered to do something for me. I thought he might be around. Do you know when he's leaving for Switzerland?"

"Well, with the airport fiasco, my advice to him was to stay home. But he's still going. He flies out Thursday night. So with the time difference, he'll land in Geneva Friday morning. Should I have him call you before he takes off, or do you just want to try his cell right now?"

"I'll try his cell. You don't need to tell him I called. I can probably manage on my own. I know he's busy. But thanks, Cindy. It was great to talk to you."

"You too, Evan. You've got to come by and see me more!"

I said I would and then we hung up. Definite crush. Obvious. A total crush on me. But I had to stay focused. Couldn't cloud my mind with the adoration of women, otherwise I'd be toast.

Anyway, bottom line was that we were ahead of Richmond. We were heading out that night, he was scheduled to head out two nights later. Not much lead time, but I was thankful that we weren't going to run into him at the airport.

S o I have to say that the airport was still **16** pretty jumpy. A lot of embarrassed police-men and security guys walking around. Everyone kind of nervous. Nothing like a bunch of TV cameras to put people on edge. Still, we didn't get a hard time. Three idiot kids. Not likely to be terrorists.

We didn't get to the airport with much time to spare—had spent every minute of the day preparing. We were flying out at eight that night, so we'd arrive in France the next morning. I was kind of hungry—wanted to get something to eat. But by the time we got through security, the plane was already board-ing. I put a portion of my $15,000 toward three large bags of cashew nuts and was on the plane stuffing my face before I knew what was happening.

And things happened just as quickly when we arrived. The flight was easy and uneventful—we mostly slept—and we hit the ground running after we landed in Paris. It was certainly on my mind to check into a swank hotel and eat caviar all day. What's better than that when you're cutting summer school? But we obviously had pressing business to get to.

In fact, the way things ended up unfolding, we really didn't do much more than drive through Paris. We jumped in a cab at the airport and told the driver to take us to the Café Saint-Beauvais. Lubchenko said he'd be gone, but we decided we should check it out. How reliable is the promise of an international spymaster?

But Lubchenko wasn't lying when he said he was splitting. I figured we'd have to go inside, ask a few questions, maybe bum-rush the waiters and storm the kitchen. But when we finally got there, we discovered that the café was completely boarded up.

"I think he's really gone," Erika said.

"Looks like it," I replied.

We asked the cab to wait for a minute and got out. Some of the windows were soaped up. Boards covered others. And there was a big piece of plywood in front of the door. We did manage to peer in through a small broken pane of glass, and the place was entirely empty. I mean, everything was gone. It was like some kind of weird urban legend—like this place had only existed in some kind of dream or belonged to some kind of phantom hitchhiker.

"Let's get out of here," I finally said. "Nothing to see."

"It's weird that there's not even a real estate agent's sign or something," Ruben said, turning back to the cab. "I guess whoever owns it doesn't even want to rent it out."

Once we hopped back in the cab, Erika gave the next destination to the cabdriver in her pristine French. It's a remarkable

fact that my French had actually gotten worse that semester—
after a trip to France. Just shows how little you can learn when
you really put your mind to it. But again, Erika's French was
excellent, and after she gave the order, we were off to the town
of Champlan, the smallish suburb south of Paris where
Lubchenko Auto was located.

I will say that the cabdriver seemed kind of annoyed when
he heard where we were going. Champlan was a hike. But it
didn't look like anyone else was trying to hail him. He just ran
his fingers through his long gray mustache and then sped south,
out of Paris. He did manage a little English along the way:
"Why in hell you go to place like Champlan! *Nossing eez zere.*"

We paused for a moment, and then I said, "Business. Just a
little business."

"Teenager business!" he said. "I don't want to know."

And that was it. No more talking. Just a pleasant and silent
ride.

S o, as is probably obvious to everyone, you 17 don't always get what you think you're getting when you buy stuff online. I, for instance,
used to sell stolen office equipment online, and
I'm pretty sure no one thought I had ripped it off
from my father. Still, despite understanding this
fact, we were all quite surprised when we arrived at
the hotel in Champlan.

"This is it?" Erika said.

"It seemed okay from the Web site," I replied. "Anyway, it
was cheap. We've got to get something back from the pawnshop, otherwise I'm dead."

"Well, it's not exactly the Ritz," Ruben said.

"Anyway, what difference does it make? We've got work to
do. We're not on some kind of cruise here." I also pointed out
that I didn't see anything else nearby—online or standing there.
I said we could jump in the cab and head back to Paris but
then suggested that we live with what we had.

"Agreed," Erika said. "But I'm making reservations from
now on."

I just shrugged. "Fine with me," I said.

The fact is that I actually kind of liked the look of the place.

It wasn't what you'd call luxurious. But it was kind of friendly looking. It was called La Royale, too, which I thought was funny.

"It has character," I finally said.

"The place is a dump," Ruben replied, and then he headed in through the front door.

The lobby was pretty big, but it was decorated with the worst, most beat-up furniture that you can imagine. Ancient stuff that looked like it was sold at a deep discount when it was brand-new. And there was dust. A lot of dust. Covered every-thing. And it was so thick in the air that you could barely see three feet in front of you—and that's no exaggeration. It was like someone had lit a fire.

Not surprisingly, the guy working the front desk also seemed to be hundreds of years old and was very strange looking—he was totally bald, except for these large clumps of ear hair that tumbled down his earlobes. Extremely weird looking. But I have to say, he was a pretty nice guy. He smiled when he saw us. Said he had been expecting us. I don't think they had too many guests.

"The Macalister group," he said. "Three rooms, I believe."

"You speak English," I said.

"I was in the French navy," he said. "And I was a liaison to the American armed forces. I lived in San Diego for five years when I was a young man."

"Huh," I said. I was kind of amazed. San Diego.

"I left the navy when I inherited this hotel from my father, although it used to be in better shape. And so did I. I'm afraid it's hard to keep things up when you get old."

I guess that's true. That's why I prefer being young. But I did like this guy.

Anyway, he showed us to our rooms, and despite how beat-up this place was, they were surprisingly enormous. Mine had a king-size bed with a series of ridges and ditches running length-wise. The mattress had no springs, and (curious about what exactly I was sleeping on) I read the tag and discovered that it was stuffed with horsehair. No joke.

"It's horsehair!" I yelled, walking into Ruben's room. "Horsehair! We're sleeping on horsehair." And then I went into Erika's room to tell her. I was pretty excited. Surprisingly, how-ever, this didn't thrill my two companions like it did me.

And now, since I've mentioned walking into "Erika's room," I will take this opportunity to discuss something important.

Careful observers might imagine that Erika and I would share a room. She was my woman, after all, and men and women often share beds. And I will say, so there's no confu-sion, that I wanted to share a room. Seemed like a perfectly logical thing to do. Share a room. Share a bed. We were going out. We were free and on our own in a foreign country. And this is what I said. "So, I figure we'll just share a room, babe," I said, as casually as I possibly could.

"Forget it," she replied.

Now, Erika was very relaxed and (unlike me) not at all uptight about anything. But she had this infuriating independent side to her, which drove me crazy because I'm into the whole devotional thing.

Anyway, she said, "Forget it," and I said, "Why forget it? It will be romantic. Don't you want a romantic trip?"

"I want space, Evan, and I need my own room. I like you more than any other guy I've ever dated. I mean it. But that doesn't mean I need you crowding around me all the time. Trust me. I'm doing this for us. You don't want to see what will happen to me if we share a room." Erika was smiling, and I've got to say that I really didn't get any negative vibes as she said this—that is, I wasn't feeling like she was addressing any deep problems in our relationship. I'm just a very needy man, as I've already pointed out, and Erika had to work very hard to keep me at bay. She even kissed me after saying all this. "I'm really happy with you, Evan," she said. "I'm really, really happy we're together. I mean it. It's the best thing that's happened to me all year. But I'm an independent person, so you can't be on top of me all the time."

I paused to consider this. Very profound and touching. Finally I said, "Please can we share a room?"

"No," she replied.

"Please?"

"No."

"Please?"

"Forget it, Evan. You're driving me crazy."

"But I want to share a room."

"No."

"Please?"

"No."

Anyway, as has been decisively established, this was a very common kind of conversation between the two of us. And the bizarre truth is that I think she found some of it kind of endearing. She'd laugh, and poke me, and then try to look angry, and then laugh again. But she never threw in the towel, as they say. She never gave in.

And here's something else I need to say. I understand that I am a bit rebellious and a bit cocky and that I am certainly irreverent and disrespectful. But in many ways, I'm a modest man, and there are certain issues that I'm not entirely comfortable talking about—perhaps evidence that my father's insane child-rearing practices have gotten the better of me. Anyway, Erika and I were going out, so let your imagination run wild. That's all I'm going to say. Really. Everything else is none of anyone's goddamned business.

Whatever.

So, we still had a lot of work to do. Things were just beginning. Richmond would soon be arriving in Switzerland, and who knew how much time we had before he swapped the virus for cash and then went after my father? Had to get moving.

T his was the plan. Go to Lubchenko Auto, have Erika sweet-talk the mechanic into telling us who his customers were that had old Mercedes, and then go to the various locations to see if we found *our* Lubchenko.

"This is ridiculous," Ruben said as we wound through Champlan in a cab we had called. "Lubchenko's long gone by now."

"We might turn up something," I said. "And if not, we'll buy some knives and go kill Richmond ourselves."

The cabdriver suddenly turned around and looked at me.

"Kidding, kidding, he's kidding," Erika said in English and in French. Then she turned and gave me a completely hostile look, which was reproduced once we arrived and got out of the cab.

"Just because you can't speak a foreign language doesn't mean other people can't," she said. "English is pretty common, Evan, especially for French cabdrivers, so watch it."

"You're right, you're right," I said. And she was right.

Anyway, Lubchenko Auto was kind of nestled in a semi-industrial area of Champlan. There were lots of warehouses, a beat-up gas station, a large, mostly empty store that sold light fixtures, a couple of old dilapidated buildings, and a couple of vacant lots. Very gritty, but in a very appealing way. Also deserted. There were one or two cars on the road and a few workmen going in and out of the buildings. But it was pretty different from Paris.

I looked around for another second and then up at the sign above the door. Lubchenko Auto, it said, unsurprisingly.

"Are we ready?" I asked.

"Ready," Ruben replied.

"I'm not," Erika said. "But that's not going to change. Let's go."

And in we went.

So, remarkably, people aren't usually very willing to let you snoop around in their offices. We asked. Very politely. We had been there before—on our last trip—so we had some idea of what to expect. But the woman we had spoken to before wasn't there. Instead, there was this hard-nosed French tough guy who told us that he wasn't letting a pack of American kids pick through his files.

"You must be out of your mind," he said to Erika. This guy was obviously going to be trouble. He was covered in grease, had these beefy fingers that could probably bend steel, and his lips were pulled back like he had just smelled rotten fish. We didn't have a chance. There was another, younger mechanic in the back. Closer to our age, and probably more susceptible to the charms of Erika. But it wasn't our luck to get him to come talk to us. Anyway, the guy we were talking to was clearly the boss, so we would have had to go through him anyway.

"It's very important," Erika said again, trying to look as innocent as possible.

"You're completely crazy. My customers expect privacy. And you could be thieves."

"Maybe if I just tell you what we're looking for?"

"Perhaps you're not understanding me, my young American friend."

"If you can just tell us about any old Mercedes you work on."

"Absolutely not."

"It's very important," Erika said again, now trying to smile as sweetly as possible.

"Absolutely not," the man said again.

Again, this was all in French, and most of it had to be reported and translated later by Erika. My F in French was a pretty good indication of how well I spoke the language. But you don't have to know much French to know what a man means when he scowls at you and screams, *"Non, non, non!"*

Still, Erika was a trouper. She did her best. She batted her eyes, pouted as though she might cry, and even touched his forearm. But this guy was a rock, and there was nothing to do but pack it in.

Erika thanked the man politely, although this was pretty pointless. The guy just glared at us as we backed out of the office. And then we were outside, right back where we started.

It was now early evening and the sun was just beginning to

set. The empty, industrial street that opened up ahead of us was surprisingly beautiful and was a pretty big contrast to all that hostility inside. Kind of made me calm down. I mean, the guy did have a point. I don't really like the idea of people snooping through private records, even if it is just the repair records of a car. Still, this was an emergency situation. Richmond was probably drinking a martini and putting in calls to his buyers, getting ready for his trip to Switzerland.

"There's only one thing to do," I finally said, looking down the long empty street before us.

"What?" Erika said, still appearing frazzled from her battle with the mechanic.

"We've got to come back after dark and break in."

"We're not breaking in," Ruben said.

"Yes we are."

"No we're not."

"Yes we are."

"No we're not."

It was a common sort of argument I had with Ruben—the sort that could normally go either way. But I knew I would win this one. Under the circumstances, we really had no choice.

S o we went back to the hotel, took showers (because, frankly, we all still smelled like airplane food), and waited till the night set in. We did a few errands as well. First we changed a lot of our American money for euros (not surprisingly, the money they use in Europe). The cashier looked at us a bit funny—not often that three teenagers hand over thousands of dollars in cash. But what could he say?

19

Next we got a pay-as-you-go cell phone and loaded it with about two hundred euros' worth of minutes. (We might need to place a few lengthy calls to a lawyer, after all.) Then we went to a big hardware store and bought a pair of industrial-strength metal clippers—the kind they use to bust into school lockers when a kid has lost his key or combination. We also grabbed three flashlights, a map to find addresses of car owners, and latex gloves so we didn't leave fingerprints. And then we went to a kind of general department store and bought a tin of black shoe polish to darken and camouflage our faces that night (we were the real thing) and several candy bars, which Ruben insisted were vital for emergency energy.

"Great," Erika said. "When we're running from the cops, I'll have chocolate to stuff in my mouth."

And after all that, we grabbed a quick bite at a small restaurant by the train station. It was a beat-up place, but the food was good. A fortunate fact of France. Even the low-grade places will serve you an excellent dinner. Finally, after eating (and killing a little more time), we headed back to Lubchenko Auto, figuring that it was now late enough for everyone to have gone home.

So, breaking into this place wasn't as hard as you'd think. I'd say that, in general, things in the lovely town of Champlan were a little sleepier than in Paris. Parts of it seemed nice—it had its mansions and expensive shops, like any town. But this was no big city, and the dangers of robbery and burglary weren't as great.

But more important, the auto shop was pretty beat-up, and it didn't really have much of a security system. There were bars on the front windows. And it even looked like there was some kind of alarm setup. But there was a big, open lot to the side of the shop where they kept a bunch of cars, and we could see through the large, iron fence that there was probably a pretty easy way into the back.

So up we went, over the fence and into the Lubchenko Auto lot. There was a half-moon out. And there were a couple of dim lights shining from the warehouse the next lot over. So we could see a little. But it was still pretty dark. And in the shadows, with all the broken-down cars in heaps next to one another, the place seemed kind of desolate.

"Kind of creepy," Erika said.

After getting our bearings for a second, we began to walk to the building. We had the metal clippers. And Ruben claimed that he could pick locks—he insisted that he had learned how online. Right. Still, it was anyone's guess how we were going to get in. But as it turned out, we didn't need any fancy equipment or expertise. As we approached the building, we quickly noticed a high window that was ajar.

"That window's open," Erika whispered.

I looked up and then said, "Boost me up," to Ruben. "I'll climb in and see if I can open the back door. If not, you guys will have to follow."

Ruben (somewhat reluctantly) bent over and I crawled up his back, kicking him several times and making a point of stepping on his head. Finally I pushed the window a few times and it swung open. Then I pulled myself up. In the next instant, I was sliding down the other wall and into the office. I flipped on my flashlight and quickly found my way to the back door. I felt around for the lock. But (quite surprisingly) as I moved my hands across the wooden door, it swung open under the pressure. It wasn't locked at all.

"It wasn't locked," I whispered as I saw Ruben and Erika on the other side of the door.

"Weird," Ruben replied, also in a whisper. "Pretty lax

around here. I guess that's the advantage of having such a beat-up office. You'll never be robbed."

Still, it was strange. Even people with nothing to lose will lock their doors. I wondered why no one had closed up properly. But in the next second, I had my answer. As I swept my flashlight across the office, I suddenly spotted something that stopped me dead in my tracks. A face—eyes shut, nose scrunched up, hands curled up under the chin, and fast asleep, and all attached to a body that was sprawled out over the ragged office couch.

"It's the guy from today," Erika whispered when she spotted him. We moved the flashlights away from him and spotted like a million empty beer bottles strewn around the floor.

At this moment, there was a sudden, loud snoring sound, some babbling, and then a hand jerked forward and knocked over one of the bottles. It didn't break, but it made quite a bit of noise. There was another snore and more babbling. But the guy didn't wake up.

"He's passed out," Ruben said. "The guy's totally drunk."

I moved the flashlight back to his face—right in his eyes, even—but he didn't wake up. He was drooling, and there was spit caked on his lips. Nice.

"He's passed out, all right," I said, still very quietly. "But let's be careful."

We then stepped past him and went back behind the counter to the file cabinets. There were about seven of them, all five drawers high. Could be a long night. But after opening one, we realized that they were organized by car make. It wasn't hard to find the Mercedes section, and that section didn't end up being that big. We pulled all the records—it was a stack about eighteen inches high—and went to the back desk. We each grabbed a chair, divided the stack three ways, and, in the next instant, we were going through the records, looking for an old Mercedes.

"What do you think 'old' means?" Erika said as she looked through the records.

"Pull anything that's over ten years and we'll go from there," I replied. "I bet it's older than ten years—some kind of antique—but let's get everything."

It actually didn't take too long. About forty-five minutes to sort through the Mercedes stack. The garage had worked on about a hundred Mercedes, and about twenty of these were over ten years old. Of these, seven were over twenty years old.

"Write down the names and addresses as well as the years," I whispered. "Lubchenko's bound to be driving a classic rather than a clunker. We'll hit the addresses of the oldest and best cars tomorrow. And if that doesn't turn anything up, we'll move down the list."

We each only had six or seven names to write down. We were almost out of there. Suddenly, just as we started writing, there was the sound of breaking glass—a bottle from near the drunk guy. We quickly turned off the flashlights. We were all motionless, hoping the guy would go back to sleep. But then another bottle was knocked over, and we heard the shuffling of feet. And then, in the next instant, the light suddenly came on.

It was a bit like what they say in nature shows—that the rattlesnake or the wolf is more afraid of you than you are of it. This mean-ass guy, covered in grease, with the permanent snarl and the thick fingers, took one look at us and let out an absolutely bloodcurdling scream. And then he paused. And then he let out another bloodcurdling scream. He was still totally drunk and was now moving very awkwardly, but in the next minute, he quickly shot off in the direction of the door that led from the office to the garage. And for a drunk guy, he didn't do that badly. He tripped over a large rolling cart that had a coffeemaker on it. But he got up quickly. And in the next instant, he was in the garage, with the door shut and locked behind him (and still screaming).

Funny how alcohol works. Some people get pretty mean. Others get deliriously happy. And others just freak out. Frankly, I didn't think this guy had it in him. I would have guessed he was entirely incapable of being so scared. But that's the way these things usually go. He was probably so pissy earlier that day because he was hungover. What a life.

But we didn't have time to comfort him. I looked up at Ruben and Erika.

"Write everything down as quickly as you can and let's get out of here," I said.

It only took a few more minutes, and before long we were done and putting the files back into the cabinet. The funny thing was that the guy kept screaming. Short bursts. Then silence. Then bursts of screaming again. It was actually kind of alarming. I almost wanted to go into the garage to comfort him. But there was no time to tend to an insane drunk man. Had to get going. And in the next minute, we headed back outside, scaled the fence, and, as quickly and discreetly as possible, left Lubchenko Auto (and the screaming Frenchman) behind.

"What a night," Ruben said as we turned a corner and set off toward the hotel. "I hope that guy doesn't try to track us down."

"He's not going to remember anything," I said. "And if he does, he's going to think he imagined it. He was pretty drunk. All that screaming. What a nightmare. But I think that was a pretty successful mission, all things considered."

"I guess," Ruben said. "But that guy still freaked me out."

Anyway, back at the hotel, we began to look over our new info. We went into my room, got out the map, and started finding the streets where the cars were. It was kind of tricky, though—they were pretty spread out. Would be hard to make good time and even harder to walk. There was probably a bus system in the town, but I had a better idea.

I went to the bedside table where the phone was and pulled out the phone book from the shelf beneath.

"Let's rent a car," I said. "I'm sure they'll open early. We can get it by seven and hit all these addresses before people head to work. And if we don't get lucky, we'll drive to Switzerland and drive the car right over Richmond's back."

"Sounds like a good idea," Ruben said.

Anyway, it didn't take long to find the names of some car rental places and to plot out a route for the next day. And then it was time for bed. We were exhausted and definitely needed sleep. All that flying, and cabbing, and breaking and entering was hard on a guy like me—I need to be comfortable at all times.

Still, was hard getting to sleep. Couldn't help but think about Richmond and smallpox and my father. Too much to contemplate. And all very real. This all may sound fun. And I may seem like a hilarious guy. But I was scared. Even if it doesn't always come through in all this. I really was scared.

A nyway.
So renting a car is actually harder than it seems. At the first place we went to, they just laughed at us. You have to be well over the legal driving age to get one. Apparently, it's too expensive to insure teenagers—a fact I find extremely offensive.

20

"That's the end of that," Ruben said, following our first humiliation.

"Let's try another place," I said.

"It's a law, Evan," Ruben said. "It's the same everywhere. The guy told us that."

Still, it seemed there would be a way. We went back to the hotel, looked through the phone book again, and found a rental car place that looked a little more low grade, a little more local, and a little more desperate for cash.

"Let's just try this place," I said.

Unfortunately, this place said the same thing.

But it was definitely a little down-at-the-heels, and the guy looked like he probably wasn't getting paid that well. So I used a little negotiation technique that I've found useful over the years. I pulled three hundred euro notes out of my stash and slipped them across the counter. Funny: most people hesitate; they don't want to appear too desperate or greedy. Not this guy. His hand slapped down on the counter and the deal was done.

"I think I can help you, Mr. Macalister," he said. "Just fill out this form and write down that you're twenty-five. And don't hit anyone because then we'll both be in lots of trouble."

After Erika translated, I said, "No problem. I'm the best driver in the state of Washington."

Erika rolled her eyes. But she translated anyway.

The man just smiled, looking not at all convinced.

Anyway, I handed him my driver's license and passport (which he photocopied), Ruben gave him his credit card, and before long, we had wheels.

So I've got to say that navigating the roads in a foreign country can be tricky. They drive on the right side of the street in France, so there wasn't too much danger there. But it's hard to figure out where you're going in a foreign place. First of all (as is probably obvious), the signs are all in French, which didn't help very much. Second, French people aren't very talented drivers. I'm sorry to say this because I tend to like French people. But it's a fact. And the third issue that I should bring up is that French people drive around in little cars—a lot like clown cars. Erika drove an SUV in Seattle, so (since my cheapskate father never got me a car) that's what I was usually carted around in. Ruben drove a Lexus that used to belong to his mom—again, Ruben was loaded, and his parents (unlike my father) shared the wealth. But the car we rented felt like something close to a cardboard box—a particularly flimsy cardboard box. And we looked like idiots too. This was no way to track down bad guys. Still, what could we do? And it was bright purple. Ridiculous, but French people paint all sorts of things weird colors. There's no explaining it.

At any rate, despite the difficulties, we found our way around town. And I've got to say, the car really turned out to be helpful. Nothing like a car for getting things done in a hurry. We zipped from address to address, trying to figure out who the owners of the various Mercedes were. But despite our rapid pace, we weren't very lucky that morning.

As usual, our technique wasn't very sophisticated. We found the address, tried to spot the car, and then walked up to the door and had Erika ask for the person. Once we saw the person, we could see whether or not we were dealing with Lubchenko.

We also came up with a backstory, just in case. "If anyone asks, you say we're looking for your long lost father," I said. "The man who deserted you and your mother when you were just a baby."

"Yeah right," Erika replied. Erika's parents, by the way, were still happily married.

"No really," I said. "We've got to say something if someone asks."

"Well I'm not saying that," she replied.

"Can you think of anything else?"

She couldn't. Neither could Ruben. And it wasn't a bad plan. It was heavy enough that no one would give us a hard time. And it also might produce some sympathy and help if we needed it.

However, for most of the morning, the story never came up. We went from address to address and found no Lubchenko. And no one really cared what we were looking for once we said, "We're sorry. We thought you were somebody else."

We said this to a bleary-eyed father of five kids, an old man who walked with crutches, a young office executive too busy to talk, a guy named Dr. Esteron who dressed like a gymnast, a man who was wearing a thick wool hat (in summer), and (apparently) a yoga instructor. Not very helpful.

There was only one place where we couldn't find anyone. A very large and elegant apartment building near the heart of Champlan. Very high end. A very beautiful old building that obviously cost a lot of money to live in. There was no answer at the downstairs buzzer, which we pressed over and over. The man's name from the car records was Henri Corpet, although there was no little nameplate by the apartment number (as there was with everyone else). Still, we kept pressing it. But no answer.

We were kind of stuck. But eventually one of the tenants left the building, and we slipped through the locked front door and into the lobby. In the next second, we jumped on the elevator and found our way to the actual apartment. And then we started knocking again.

But no luck. No one was home. We knocked for about five minutes (although this seemed pretty hopeless).

Finally Erika said, "This is ridiculous. There's no one home."

"We can come back in a little bit," I replied. Kind of disappointing. But just then, a neighbor opened her door and stepped out. She was wearing a pretty nice business-type suit and carrying a black leather briefcase. She was a little surprised to see us there. And when she saw us standing outside the door to the Corpet residence, she said in French even I understood, "There's nobody home. He moved away."

"How long ago?" Erika quickly asked.

"Are you Americans?" the woman said, now speaking English with a fairly thick accent.

"Yes," I replied. "Do you know Mr. Corpet?"

"What do you want with him?"

We froze. Finally I said, "I'm afraid it's personal."

The woman looked at me and said, "Well, I'm not sure I can tell you anything, then."

"I think he might be my father," Erika blurted out, in a very convincing tone of desperation. And the woman looked very startled by this.

"I see," she said. "Well, he moved away a few months ago. I haven't seen him since."

"Did he leave behind an address?"

"Not with me. He was kind of reclusive. But maybe the concierge has something." (*Concierge* is a fancy French word for a building superintendent.) "You should check with him. But I think he might be out for the day."

"Thanks," Erika said, trying to look like a long lost daughter.

Then I said, "Can you tell us what he looked like? Just so we know we're on the right track. There are lots of Henri Corpets in France, believe it or not."

"I can imagine," she said. "Very large, dark hair, a big mustache, and scars on his face."

I looked at Erika and Ruben.

Lubchenko.

But he had moved away.

Months ago.

"Thanks a lot," Erika finally said.

"Do you think it's him?" the woman asked.

"I think so," Erika said, again still trying to look very serious.

"Well, good luck," the woman said, and then headed down the stairs.

We stood there for a second.

Finally Ruben said, "So he's gone."

"We already figured that would be likely," I replied. "But

let's find the concierge. Maybe he left some kind of forwarding address. Or there might be some other information
about him."

In the next instant, we were headed to the stairs. Bad news
that Lubchenko had split, but this was the first lead of the day,
and we suddenly had much more energy.

21

So it's funny how friendships change. Or, it's funny how people change and their friendships follow. When I first started hanging out with Ruben, we were about seven—in second grade—and he was big for his age, if that's possible to imagine. He was always a nice guy, so it's not like he was any kind of bruiser. But when minor disputes came up—say, some tough guy in class wanted to take my juice box—Ruben always stepped in to sort things out. We went to the same school then—a Seattle public school that sat somewhere between his house and mine—and I've got to say that we were a pretty natural fit. Can't say why, but we just liked hanging around with each other, and since I was already starting to get into trouble (with teachers and juice box snatchers), he was an excellent ally.

But I was a good friend too, and as we descended the stairs at the apartment building in Champlan, for some reason I started to remember one of the first times we really bonded—bonded in an emotional way, not in a defeating-the-playground-bully kind of way. Don't really know why I thought of it, but it probably had something to do with the story we had made up for Erika.

Anyway, Ruben's parents, who are completely happily married, were having some kind of trouble. It happens. Even in happy families. His dad was away on business too much, and there was a lot of arguing, and one day Ruben showed up at my back door crying, telling me his parents were getting separated and probably getting divorced. This, by the way, was when I was about ten—the winter before my mother got sick.

Now, it may seem that I'm hardly the kind of guy you'd turn to for emotional advice. But as we sat at my kitchen table and he told me about what had happened—his father had packed a bag and split for some hotel—I just kind of sat there and listened and said what I could to calm him down. It's hard. There's not really a right thing to say. But sometimes people just need you to sit there and nod, and I was pretty good at that.

We were alone. My mom was out and Dad was at work. Mrs. Andropolis, our housekeeper, was upstairs watching television—she had several afternoon programs she never missed—and she didn't really know Ruben was over. I'm sure she would have made him eat some kind of nut-and-honey cake (her Greek solution for all kinds of trauma and sadness). But for a while, it was just me. Anyway, hardly an act of heroism on my part, but that day kind of has a lot attached to it. I know I was young, but I remember feeling very adult at that moment, trying to sort through what was in fact a very real problem in my best friend's life. And I remember feeling like I was helping, like

I was being a good friend. It was kind of my first real memory of that sort of feeling, and it suddenly seemed significant on those stairs in Lubchenko's apartment building in France.

But the memory was pretty full, pretty packed, and as we got closer to the ground floor, what I remembered most about that day was my dad. He came home early, as Ruben and I were sitting together in the kitchen. He was traveling the next day and needed to pack and get some things ready from his office at home. He walked in the back door, kind of talking to himself about something, and then suddenly halted when he saw Ruben sitting at the table crying.

I was saying something to Ruben, but at that moment my attempts to console him weren't working that well—I mean, a parents' potential divorce isn't exactly an easy thing to resolve at a kitchen table. Anyway, my dad already had something of a reputation among my friends for being a grouch, and when he walked in, Ruben quickly wiped away his tears and tried to compose himself. Didn't really work, but he also wasn't blubbering anymore. The amazing thing, though, was how my dad reacted. I could have an iron bolt lodged in my brain, and my father would tell me to stop complaining and act like a man. But this isn't what he did with Ruben.

"What's going on?" he said. "Are you all right, Ruben?"

Ruben wasn't quite sure how to respond, but he finally said, "I think my parents are getting divorced."

My dad paused for a moment and then said, "I'm sorry to

hear that." Then he sat down at the table and asked Ruben to tell him more.

I've got to say it was kind of touching—this hard-ass guy suddenly looking so concerned. And the thing was that it was real. He was genuinely moved by Ruben's tears. And it was most strange because my father's kindness seemed to work. Ruben told his story, and my father listened patiently, and Ruben seemed to relax a bit. And my father gave good advice—he kept saying things like, "I'm so sorry you've had to go through this." And, "I know that your parents love each other and that they love you, so I'll bet things will come out all right in the end." And, "Sometimes people just need to get it all out of their system. I wouldn't be surprised if all this blows over by the end of the month." (It did, in fact, blow over by the end of the month.)

Anyway, it was all strange. It was strange to see my father able to comfort Ruben like that. I was impressed. Kind of proud. But it did also occur to me that this was a side of my father that I almost never saw. And maybe for the first time in my life, I was wondering why he wasn't like that more with me. I was still young at that point. Ten, like I said. So I hadn't really begun my slide into deepest delinquency. But the signs of my future were already appearing, and my dad was already trying the tough approach to rein me in.

And when things went south in my life (like failing my first classes) I got the "stop complaining and get on with it" talk.

Granted, I'd never really faced anything like a divorce. Up till that point, nothing seriously bad had ever happened. But the thing is that it was about to. My mother got sick that spring, and by August she was dead. Hard to beat that for tragedy. But through it all, I got almost none of what my dad gave Ruben that day. It may have been harder for my dad to deal with. Not the kind of thing where you can say, "It'll turn out all right. You just wait and see. Just give it a month." In fact, there's almost nothing you can say. It's such an inscrutable moment—such an unexplainable event—that no one ever really knows what to say or how to act. Especially with a kid around. Hard to know how to treat a ten-year-old after that. My dad's reaction mostly seemed to be that he and I had a long road ahead of us, and we had to get tough quick, and a young boy who's lost his mother wasn't going to benefit from a lot of weeping and hugging. Life was as real as it gets at that point, and my father's solution was to grit his teeth and get on with things. Again, I can't blame him. It seems like a logical response. Lose your mother and you get pretty terrified about the way life can unfold. It seems reasonable that my dad reacted with discipline and toughness. Still, the problem with this solution is that it was a kind of lie. There was no way to tough it out where losing my mother was concerned. Hugging and weeping is really about all you're capable of when something like that happens, and to pretend otherwise just kind of aggravates the pain.

Whatever. Maybe this is all unimportant. Maybe all my

complaints about my father really are the "nonsense" my dad said I was prone to carry on about. But all this was kind of on my mind, at least in a larger kind of way. I was in a tough situation. Maybe I was going to be shot and killed the next day—I really thought about my father and me and what a rotten time we'd had of it. I mean, the fact is that I always knew my father loved me. He was a brute to me, but he loved me. The thing is that he seemed to love me out of a sense of duty, rather than any kind of real understanding, or out of any kind of joy I brought him. And love earned purely through duty—not out of happiness or understanding—isn't very satisfying. It occurred to me, in fact (again, in a flash, on those stairs in Champlan), that if my father weren't my father and I met him at some kind of social gathering (some picnic or dinner) and we talked about our lives, he'd come to the conclusion that I was not at all the kind of person he liked. And that was pretty strange—to feel loved and not liked.

Whatever. Again, maybe my dad was right—maybe all this sentimental nonsense should be forced out of your mind, not indulged and brooded over. Still, it was hard not to think about it all. I don't know. This sudden series of strange feelings about my friends just came to me. It's not like I decided to have these thoughts. Anyway. Like I said, whatever.

B ack to the story.

22

We arrived downstairs, back in the lobby, and started to look for the concierge's office. It was pretty easy to find since it was marked with a big brass nameplate that said Concierge. Unfortunately, there was a note, scrawled across a piece of notebook paper. It said he would be out for the day and wouldn't be back till five. The reason? The note said he was "in Paris buying shoes."

"What kind of country is this?" I said. "Are there no shoe stores in Champlan?"

"This is a very mysterious country," Ruben replied.

"Well, I guess we've just got to come back," I said. "We're definitely in the right place. We've just got to wait till this evening and hope he can help us out."

Erika looked like she was trying to come up with another plan. But in the end, there wasn't much to say. It sucked. It was around 1 p.m. Richmond would be leaving that day for Switzerland. But still, we had to wait. Nothing else for it.

Anyway, we putzed around for a while—basically just walking in circles and eating pastries—and then went back at three, just in case the guy got back early. We did the same at four and then at four thirty. No luck. Finally, when we showed up at five (just like the note said), we buzzed the concierge's office from the outside, and in a few seconds a voice came over the intercom.

"Allo, oui?"

Erika quickly said hello and asked if we could come in to see him. In the next moment, a buzzer sounded and the door clicked open.

As we walked into the lobby, the door down at the end of the hall opened, and out stepped a fairly large man wearing a kind of blue workman's coat. I was kind of shocked when I saw him. He was an older guy. All gray, with wrinkles. And he was heavy—like he ate way too much. Not at all the kind of guy you'd imagine heading into the big city on a shoe-shopping expedition.

I guess Ruben was thinking the same thing. "This guy went shoe shopping in Paris?" he said.

"I know," I replied. "Very strange."

But the man actually turned out to be very nice. He invited us into his small living room—behind the door marked Concierge was an apartment, not an office. And when we sat down, he smiled politely and asked if we'd like anything to drink.

"Perhaps you are thirsty?" he said, in slow French that I could sort of make out. Kind of inspiring, really—we're three young strangers and he just invites us in for drinks. In the

United States, we would have been shot before we made it through the front door.

At any rate, Erika explained why we were there—we were looking for a man named Henri Corpet.

"What would you like with him?" he asked, with no suspicion, but with appropriate respect for his tenants' privacy.

Again, dicey, especially since this guy seemed so nice and gentle. Hated to lie to him. But the prospect of a world smallpox plague will lead you to do all sorts of things. So Erika repeated her story—that she thought he might be her father. She even expanded the story in a fairly unexpected way.

"He was an artist, a painter, living in Baltimore," she said. "That's where he met my mother. They fell in love, and then he left her. And me. It was heartbreaking."

I was fairly shocked by this sudden literary flourish (after she translated it for me). I thought I was the only one who knew how to lie like that. Something to remember. Not good having a girlfriend who's a talented liar.

The concierge (who we can now call Monsieur Plessix, because that's how he introduced himself) was also impressed. Of course, he had no idea it was a lie. But he was kind of moved.

"I don't know the man very well myself," he said, stroking his chin. "But if he has done this, then I am very sorry. But he left. Two months ago. And I don't believe he left a forwarding address."

Then Mr. Plessix paused for a moment and said, "But let me check the apartment file."

He got up, went to a small chest of drawers, and pulled out the top one. There were several stacks of manila files piled one on top of another. A fairly crude system, but it seemed to get the job done. After looking through one of the stacks, he pulled out a file with a large 43 written on the top—Lubchenko's apartment number—and walked back to where we were sitting.

"Perhaps there will be something in here that can help you," he said.

But there wasn't. No address, no ID, no nothing.

"He was an unusual man," Mr. Plessix finally said. "He paid for the entire year ahead of time—in cash. So there are no bank statements of any kind." Then he paused again and looked over at Erika. "I'm so sorry," he said. "I'm sure you'll find him."

It was kind of touching. He was really sincere. Again, made me feel kind of guilty that we were lying to him. But what choice did we have? Anyway, that was that. It looked like we were pretty much stuck.

We stood up, Mr. Plessix apologized again, and then we began to move toward the door. But at that moment, Mr. Plessix apparently thought of something. "Wait here for just a second," he said suddenly. "I've just remembered some-thing."

He went to another room and came out with a large card-board box, filled with all sorts of junk. He put the box down on a small table in the entryway and began looking through it.

"These are just odds and ends I keep," he said. "But I think I have something of his. If you find him, maybe you can give it to him."

He picked up a large, leather-bound book and opened it up. He flipped through the pages for a second, and then he pulled out an envelope that was stuck near the back.

"This came after he left," he said. "He left no forwarding address, so I couldn't send it to him. Maybe you can pass it along."

Then he handed Erika the envelope. I almost snatched it out of her hands but managed to keep my cool. Instead, I just thanked Mr. Plessix again. Erika and Ruben did the same. And in the next minute, we were walking through the lobby and then out the front door.

I t felt like a long walk to the car because we were trying not to make too much of a scene over the envelope, but we were all really curious.

"What does it look like?" I asked Erika, who was discreetly looking down at the letter.

"Well, it's definitely not junk mail," she said. "It's a letter. Hand-addressed. And I'd say it's from a woman, given the loopy writing. Kind of a sexist observation. But I bet I'm right."

Now I really wanted to look at it. But I kept my cool. Until we got back in the car, when I (somewhat rudely) grabbed it from Erika.

"Hello!" Erika said. "How about some manners?"

"Sorry," I said, looking at it. Then I said, "I think we should open it."

But there was a bit of hesitation from all of us.

"It *is* someone else's mail," Erika finally said.

And this is kind of what I was thinking. Kind of strange. This was an emergency—if there was ever a reason to open someone's mail, this was it. Still, it was actually hard to open. Finally, though, we went ahead. We had no choice.

23

The letter was in French, and I could make out a little of it. But we didn't have time for me to fumble around with my terrible French, so I handed it to Erika and she translated. This is what it said:

Dear Anton,

I know I'm not supposed to write you, but I miss you very much. I wonder when you are going to return, and I hope that it's soon. The peach trees are in bloom, and I know this is your favorite time of year in the south. Perhaps you will finish your business in time to see the flowers you planted last year along the front path. I guess I'm just trying to tell you that I miss you, and that I've been counting the days until you return home.

Love, Christina

Frankly, it was kind of touching. When you're reading the mail of an international freedom-fighting soldier, you expect coordinates and descriptions of bombs, not a love letter.

Ruben remarked on the other strange news: "Lubchenko's name is Anton?"

"I know," I replied. "Strange that he's got a real name."

I flipped the envelope over and looked at the address again. It was mailed to Henri Corpet. Definitely someone assuming a false identity. More important, though, given what we had just read, there was a return address: 274 Rue du Chalutier, St.-Tropez.

"Where the hell is Saint-Tropez?" I said.

"It's in the south," Erika said. "On the Mediterranean Sea. Lubchenko must be pretty fancy. Saint-Tropez is where movie stars hang out."

"Why don't I know about it?" I said.

"Because, my friend," Ruben said, "despite what you may think, you are not a movie star."

"But I will be."

"Right. Right. You will be."

We all sat there for a moment, a bit confused. And then I stated what had to be the obvious conclusion at that point. "I'm betting this return address is where Lubchenko lives. At least part of the time. If he's planting flowers along the 'front path,' he's got to spend some time there. And the writer did say 'return home.'" I paused for a moment and then said, "I guess we're heading to Saint-Tropez."

Ruben and Erika just looked at me. They looked like they wanted to resist, but they knew I was right. We had to head south.

24

S o we quickly discussed logistics on the drive back to the hotel. The first thought was to rush to the airport and fly down. But then we decided to drive it. It was a hike—probably eight hours—but who knew if we could get plane tickets that late? And with all the arrangements and getting to the airport, etc., it seemed best to just jump on the road as quickly as possible. More important, we might not get so lucky at another car rental place, and holding on to a car seemed pretty important.

"Anyway," I said, "a road trip will be more fun."

"Right," Erika said, squinting at me. "But not too much fun."

So, it was about five thirty when we read that letter. We went to our hotel and settled up, and by six fifteen we were on the road, headed south. Our estimated time of arrival would be about 2 a.m. We figured we'd take turns driving and sleeping so we wouldn't be too dead when we arrived.

"And I'll find us a hotel," Erika said as we got onto the highway. She started flipping through a guidebook we had brought along. After looking through the Saint-Tropez section for a few minutes, she opened the cell phone and began making calls.

"We might as well stay on the beach," she said. "Supposed to be pretty nice down there."

"I'm for that," I replied.

"I hate the beach," Ruben said.

"The beach it is, then," Erika said.

But it was actually a tall order this late in the game. It was summer, and this was a fashionable beach town. So it took some work. And some cash. Kind of upset me, actually. "I'd still like to buy back at least a few items from the pawnshop," I said. But nothing in Saint-Tropez is cheap, so I was kind of out of luck.

Eventually Erika found something—a pretty swank place that just had a cancellation. But there was only one room available, and it only had a double bed, although they said they'd wheel in a cot.

"I'm not sleeping on a cot," Ruben said.

"Well you're not sleeping with my woman," I replied.

"I might sleep with your woman."

"You're getting the cot."

It went on like this for a few minutes until Erika said, "I'll make this easy, guys. I'll take the cot."

"Whoa," I said. "I'm not sleeping with Ruben either."

"Yeah, no way," Ruben agreed. "That's definitely out."

"Look, this isn't vacation, guys. We're lucky to be getting any sleep at all. Remember there's a guy out there who wants to kill us."

"Sleeping in a bed with Ruben would be worse than getting killed. I'm sorry, but I have to put my foot down on this one."

"I agree," Ruben said, "although most people find sleeping with me totally fine. It's sleeping with you that would be painful."

Anyway, the conversation went on like this for a while, and then we drifted into silence. And then a new subject was brought up. One of the reasons road trips are great is that you really get to know your friends better. For instance, I had forgotten that Ruben's bladder was the size of a shot glass. But this is something I quickly learned.

"I have to pee," Ruben said. "Badly."

"We've only been in the car for forty minutes," I yelled.

"Maybe so," Ruben said. "But I really have to pee."

"Why didn't you go at the hotel?"

"I didn't have to then."

"But you have to now?"

"Yeah, I have to now. Badly."

"Erika, hand him an empty water bottle."

"What?"

"I'm not stopping, Ruben."

"I'm not peeing in a bottle."

"I'm afraid you'll have to."

"I'm not doing it, Evan."

"Well, I'm not stopping."

"You're stopping."

I paused for a second. Wanted to let the joke last just a minute longer. But then I started to feel bad. "Okay, okay," I finally said. "We'll stop."

There was a roadside rest stop about three miles ahead, and I pulled in as soon as we reached it. The sad fact is that I too have a fairly small bladder and spent most of my childhood getting yelled at for it by my father. So I couldn't torture Ruben for too long. I am a very sensitive man.

Anyway, we pulled over at the rest stop, and I have to say that it actually wasn't such a bad idea. I was pretty hungry, and we totally loaded up on junk food—got to have lots to eat if you're going to enjoy yourself on the road.

I have to say that French junk food is kind of a culinary event of a very high caliber. They're geniuses with food. Everyone knows that. But who would have imagined that they'd be so good with things like potato chips and candy? My favorite thing was these bacon-flavored chips that came in the shape of little pieces of bacon. We have them in the States, but they're dog treats. Anyway, they're delicious. Bacon in a bag.

"You're going to die," Erika said as we were walking out. I was pushing a fistful of the bacon chips into my mouth, and, apparently, this disturbed her.

"Will you miss me?" I said.

"No, Evan, I'll be very relieved," she said, but she was kind of laughing.

Anyway, there's not much to say about the rest of the trip.

We stopped for Ruben to pee like twenty-nine times. I ate bacon chips all the way down. Erika and Ruben drove some, and we all got some sleep. But there really wasn't much to see. It was dark, after all, and most countries look the same on the open road in the dark. Not very poetic, but a fact. The only good thing about not seeing much is that for the first time I didn't feel so foolish in our ugly little purple car.

"I'm glad no one can see how stupid we look in our purple car," I said at about the halfway mark. No response. Louder, "I said, 'I'm glad no one can see how stupid we look in our purple car.'"

"Evan, we're sleeping," Erika said.

"I'm lonely," I replied.

"I can't believe I go out with you."

"I can't believe you do either," Ruben said from the back.

"Believe it, buddy."

No response this time.

It was funny. As I was sitting there in the dark, driving south, it kind of struck me as odd that we still all got along so well together now that Erika and I were going out. Our gang of three was pretty much intact even though a central fact about it had changed. I mean, me going out with Erika could have caused a lot of problems. Still, I couldn't help but think that life would be even better if things *had* changed a little bit and certain people started being a *lot* nicer to me.

"You know," I finally said, once again breaking the silence.

"Now that I think about it, I *don't* really like the way I've been treated since Erika and I started going out. You guys kind of gang up on me."

"You deserve it," Ruben said.

"Yeah," Erika said. "You deserve it. Now please, shut up and let us get some sleep."

I still had more to say on this matter. But I decided that maybe they did, in fact, need some sleep.

Anyway, for some reason, something else suddenly hit me. This was bad stuff we were facing. It really was. A fun road trip. But bad stuff in the background. I was hopeful that Lubchenko could sort everything out. If anyone could, it was him. But still, there was a lot riding on this. And sitting in the dark, with my friends asleep, I really started to wonder if we were going to make it through everything. It was a puzzle. An imponderable one.

Still, I had plenty of bacon chips. So there was some hope.

25

W e pulled into the hotel at about two in the morning and were totally beat. It was a pretty deluxe place—a far cry from La Royale. It was called l'Archange, and there was still some activity at that hour. Bellhops, waiters, and assistant managers were still rushing around. Half-drunk old people were getting home for the evening. Twenty-somethings in slinky clothes headed in and out of the bar. And it was all accompanied by that unmistakable smell of salt air and suntan lotion. My kind of scene. But not everyone shared my point of view.

"I hate the beach," Ruben said (again).

"What are you talking about?" I said, putting my arm around his shoulders. "This is one of the best places you've ever been."

Ruben sneezed. "I'm allergic. It smells funny. And there's a constant draft. I don't like it."

Erika got behind him and pushed him forward. "We're here and you're going to like it," she said.

"I'll stay," Ruben said. "But I won't like it."

Anyway, we checked in and brought our bags up to the room. But it was so cramped in the room with three of us and there was so much fun going on downstairs that I almost started crying.

"I'm not sleeping with Ruben," I said.

"Boys, get it together," Erika finally yelled. "You're sharing a bed, and you're going to stop complaining. You think I like being in here with you two losers? Well, I don't. But you don't hear me complaining about it, do you?"

"I'm not a loser," I said. "Don't lump me in with Ruben."

"Evan, you're a loser. True, one that I like a lot. But you're just as much of a loser as Ruben."

"See," Ruben said.

"All right," I said. "Let's go down to the bar." (As you may know, there's not really a drinking age in France.)

"We've got to stay on track," Erika said. "It's two thirty a.m. We've got a big day tomorrow."

"Just for half an hour!"

"No."

"Half an hour."

"No."

"Please. Half an hour."

"Absolutely not."

So, as may be obvious, I always lose this kind of argument. Still, hard for me not to make it. The most fashionable resort town in France and we were going to spend our first night piled together in a small hotel room? I don't think so.

"Please?" I said after another pause.

"No!" This time Erika sounded a little pissed.

Another pause.

"Are you mad at me?" I finally said.

"No."

"Are you sure?"

"Yes."

"So you're not mad at me?"

"No."

"No, you're not mad, or no, you are mad?"

"Evan."

"What?"

"Stop it!"

"Now are you mad at me?"

No answer. I had more to say, but (with unusual perception) I realized that I'd better drop it. You can only push people so far, even when you're going out with them.

Anyway, Erika (and Ruben) were right about the bar. Too much was at stake the next day. As I lay there in bed, I thought about Mr. Richmond arriving in Switzerland early the following morning. I wanted to be the kind of guy who could party all night and then save the world the following morning. But my head was now feeling very heavy, and my eyes were sore, and at that moment, all I wanted was to go to sleep. Sleeping alongside Ruben didn't even seem that bad to me. And that's saying something.

"You guys are right," I finally said. "We need to sleep."

But there was no response, except for the opening moments of what would be a long night of Ruben snoring. Still, even that didn't bother me for too long, and in the next instant, I was fast asleep.

26

We were on a tough deadline, but we were dead exhausted, so we decided to sleep till eleven, which actually isn't that late given the fact that we didn't fall asleep till four. True, the future of the planet was hanging in the balance. But none of us felt like we could achieve much if we were too tired. Anyway, early in the morning was no time to pay our surprise visit to Lubchenko.

And I have to say I ended up sleeping pretty well, despite the obvious cataclysmic problems I was facing (including Ruben's snoring). And when I woke up, I felt pretty refreshed. Was ready to go. But I was also totally starving. I think all that junk food didn't actually find its way into my body. Ruben seemed to feel the same way. As I was lying (unbelievably) next to him in the bed, trying to get my bearings, he yelled, "I'm starving."

"Me too," Erika said from the cot.

"Okay, I am too," I said. "We should get lunch. But let's make it quick. We can get some kind of sandwich and eat it on the beach."

I actually would have liked to have spent the whole day on the beach. It was really a shame. I'm the kind of guy who appreciates luxury. And as I got out of bed and looked out of the hotel room window, I could tell Saint-Tropez was the real thing. My kind of place. Palm trees. Expensive Italian sports cars. Men in white tuxedos running around serving drinks. If there had been just a little more time (if there had been just one less madman bent on killing me), then maybe I could have spent the day working on my tan—one of the few things I'm good at. But no such luck.

"Okay, okay," I finally said, my nose pressed up against the hotel room window. "Got to get moving." I ran my fingers through my hair and found my pants, and in about ten minutes, we were all in the lobby, feeling pretty lousy about not being able to enjoy it all.

Still, we had time for a sandwich. And I was determined to enjoy it. And all this brings me to a FAIRLY REMARKABLE DISCOVERY I made in that noontime sun of Saint-Tropez.

So let me say by way of a preface to my explanation of this so-called remarkable discovery that I'm the kind of guy who tries to be comfortable with things like nature and the human body. I like to be in touch with myself. I work to be at ease with things like bodily functions, the human form, and natural feelings and instincts. Still, as in touch as I try to be, I'm actually a little shy. And it's very hard for me to describe certain things because, in fact, I am such a modest man. So I'm going to make this quick and let the powers of imagination fill in the blanks. Here it is: in the south of France, on beaches, some women go topless. I know. A stunning (and somewhat alarming) fact. And like I said, truly remarkable. Hard to believe that this happens in our civilized world. But it's true. And frankly, I really don't have much more to say. Surely I don't need to describe the flabbergasting astonishment that Ruben and I felt as we walked onto the seemingly normal beach in Saint-Tropez. Frankly, we didn't know what hit us as we stood there in our jeans and sneakers trying to unwrap our sandwiches. Ruben and I were totally stunned.

Erika, however, was still standing firmly in the real world, and, in fact, had a few remarks to make. She stood there for a few seconds taking in the scene. She stared at the glittering beach, edged by graceful palm trees. She looked up at a single fluffy cloud that passed overhead. She cast her gaze across the rows and rows of beautiful people, all framed by the deep blue Mediterranean Sea. Then she looked over at Ruben and me like she couldn't imagine being with a bigger pair of idiots. (Again, needless to say, both of us were blushing, slack-jawed, and starting to sweat.) She looked back at the beach—and the numerous so-called topless women. Then she looked at us again and said, "All right, guys. Get a good look and make your stupid comments. Then shut up. If you think I'm going to travel around the south of France listening to you talk about boobs the whole time, you're out of your mind. So go ahead. Get it out of your system. Start talking."

I had quite a few comments to make. I really did. Yep, lots

of things popped into my head at that moment. But just because Erika said we could get it out of our system didn't mean anything. It could have been a trap. Or she could have suddenly changed her mind. Any number of things could have happened. This is a thing I had learned with Erika. If it seemed like it was going to get you in trouble, don't do it, even if she says it's okay. And I imagine this small lesson applies to all girlfriends, especially if you're sitting on a sunny beach covered with half-naked women. This is one of the few true and undeniable things that I know about the world.

So, needless to say, I kept my mouth shut. So did Ruben. He also knew what was good for him. But Erika wasn't buying it.

"You know what," she finally said, "I'm going to sit over there under that palm tree and eat my sandwich. You just eat your lunch right here and soak up the atmosphere on your own for a few minutes. After I'm done eating, I'll come get you. I trust you'll have had your fun by then." Then Erika turned and walked away. "I've had it with this," she said, and then, a little louder, "And I definitely need to find a new boyfriend."

I wanted to protest. But somehow, I was rooted there, right in that spot in the sand. Speechless, trying to eat my sandwich, which was harder than you'd think. Finally (after what seemed like eighteen hours) Ruben said, "This is unbelievable. It's like we're on some kind of mysterious planet. I know we're in trouble here with Richmond and smallpox and every-thing, but I don't know if I can leave, Evan. I don't think I'm strong enough. I'm a weak man, Evan. You know that. I'm very, very weak."

"I'm weak too," I replied. "I'm trying to be mature. I really am. Look at me. I'm trying to behave like a grown-up. I'm try-ing. Look."

"We're just men, Evan," Ruben said after a pause. "We have to accept our limitations."

"Maybe you're right, Ruben. We're just two men. Just how much can be expected of us in this crazy, mixed-up world?"

"We try."

"We do try."

"We struggle against the darkness."

"But then, there it is again. And it's hard to pull away."

"Very hard."

"Almost impossible."

Whatever. Anyway, as embarrassed as I am to admit it (and I really am embarrassed), I'd have to say that was one of the most absorbing sandwiches I've ever eaten in my life.

But we were rescued. Finally.

After another stretch of nervous staring, Erika came back over to us. "All right, studs," she said, "time to get a move on. You've had your fun. Now let's go find Lubchenko. Say good-bye to your new friends."

Ruben and I looked around, actually feeling like we should

say good-bye. Erika just grabbed our arms and started pulling us back to the hotel. "It's a figure of speech, guys. If you start saying good-bye to everyone, you're going to get arrested."

This was probably a good point.

Anyway, we really did have to get back to the hotel to come up with a plan.

27

O kay. Here was the plan.

But let me just make one point first—something I need to restate because it addresses the fact of us being stupid and foolish enough to try to handle all this on our own. Going to the cops was a hard thing for us. We got involved in this whole disastrous episode in my life because I stole office equipment from my father's company, including a laptop with some important information about this smallpox deal. If we went to the cops, they'd find out I had stolen office equipment, so I (and Ruben, who was my accomplice) would get way busted.

Whatever, I say this because we started getting nervous about actually going to Lubchenko's house and soliciting his help. Lubchenko might be fighting for the good guys (at least as far as we knew), but the fact that he was fighting anyone or anything at all didn't really bode well for us. A lot of bad operators in his world. And Lubchenko already told us that he was a pretty single-minded guy. He didn't let his feelings get in the way of his aspirations. In other words, if three stupid American kids started interfering with something he was working on, he'd take us out of the picture pretty quickly and wouldn't feel too bad about it. I mean, we trusted Lubchenko. We did. He had helped us out before. But just because you trust someone doesn't mean you don't want to take precautions. Anyway, we came up with something of a plan. Ruben was going to stay behind and sit by the phone in the hotel room. We were going to check in every so often from our cell phone. If there was no call for two hours, Ruben would know we were in trouble. And at that point, we'd cut our losses and Ruben would go to the cops with our whole sordid story—including a detailed account of our thievery, if necessary.

"So is the plan clear?" I said to Ruben.

"How come I always have to do stuff like this?" Ruben asked.

"Would you prefer to come with us and face Lubchenko?"

"No."

"Then count your blessings."

Ruben grumbled something at me under his breath that I can't imagine was very polite.

"But don't panic if we're a little late. We'll call from the mobile every hour. If we're out of contact for more than that, get help."

"From the cops," Ruben said.

"From the cops," I repeated. "The local Saint-Tropez cops. Tell them we've been kidnapped. We'll sort it all out later. If it's a false alarm, we're just three stupid kids playing around. If not, well, then, hopefully we'll be saved."

"And the cops will want to know how we got involved in all this," Ruben said.

"Yes. Well, maybe. But one way or another, it's better than getting a knife jammed in our necks."

Anyway, that was the plan. Or, that was the precaution. The plan was to find Lubchenko and get him to help us on the Richmond thing.

According to the map, Lubchenko (we hoped) lived on a little winding road on a hill overlooking the Mediterranean. We weren't sure exactly what we were in for as we drove up the hill—did international spymasters live in mansions or shacks? Hard to say. But after checking out the houses on this road, it became pretty clear that we were in a plush neighborhood. Every house seemed to be high-end fantasy lodging for the rich and famous. Really. Every kind of whim and fancy was represented on this street. Wide bungalows covered with ivy and creeping roses. Medieval-castle-like structures with turrets and stained glass windows. Round, domed buildings painted light green and surrounded by waterfalls and hidden pools. You name it, it was on this street.

But there were other houses. Ones that were definitely owned by rich dudes but that seemed just a bit less silly. And after climbing the hill for about ten minutes, now above a breathtaking view of the village of Saint-Tropez below (and the sea beyond), we arrived at 274 Rue du Chalutier and at Lubchenko's normal but still stunning mansion.

"And I thought you lived in an impressive house," Erika said

28

as I parked at the side of the road. She turned around and then gasped, "Look at the view, Evan. I think we should see if Lubchenko will adopt us. I really think I want to live here. Forever."

I looked around, trying to take it all in as we sat there in the car. It was definitely impressive. No question about that. Lubchenko's house was this beautiful white villa, with blue shutters and a red terra-cotta roof. Surrounding it was a jungle of flowers and a huge swimming pool that was perfectly nestled into the middle of the garden.

"I should go into the freedom-fighting racket," I said. "This is the life."

"It really is," Erika replied.

Anyway, we sat there for another second, and then Erika finally said, "All right. Time to go."

"Time to go," I replied, and got out of the car.

29

S o, despite the inviting and warm look of the place, it was actually pretty hard to get in. Lots of security. Or, an iron fence around the place (with creeping flowers growing up it) and a locked gate at the end of the front path. There was a buzzer there, and a camera, and after taking a few deep breaths, I pushed the button.

A moment passed, and then a woman's voice came over the speaker: "Allo?"

Erika took over. Said we were looking for Anton—the name on the letter.

"Who is it, please?" the woman said, still in French, though.

Erika answered again, giving our names.

"Please wait for a moment."

So we did. And it was quite a moment. I'd say, in fact, that it was more like ten minutes. But finally, the same voice came over the speaker and invited us in.

"Please come in so I may talk to you," she said, now in English. A kind of airy English, with a delicate French accent. Kind of beautiful, really. And when we walked through the gate (which now popped open), and then up the winding stone path to the house, the door opened, and I saw the woman who went along with the voice. Have to say that if I had to imagine what kind of woman Lubchenko would be with, this was her. A tall, athletic, graceful, extremely healthy-looking specimen of European refinement. Long dark hair, tanned skin, and big brown eyes. She had the kind of look that would have worked whether she was a princess or the wife of a local fisherman—that is, aristocratic without looking unnatural or inaccessible.

"Hello, Evan. Hello, Erika," she said as we approached.

"Hi," we both said, a little intimidated.

"I'm Christina. It's nice to meet you."

"It's nice to meet you," Erika said, now with a little more confidence. But I was just getting more nervous.

"It's nice to meet you," I said, suddenly halting. I couldn't call her Christina. And not just because she was an adult. It wasn't like she was some kind of parent. More like she was a movie star. Like, I'd call Nicole Kidman "Ms. Kidman" if I met her because, obviously, I'm just some freak kid from Seattle who has no business talking to her in the first place. Anyway, unexplainably, and much to my embarrassment, I finished the sentence with "Miss Christina." And then I repeated the whole thing, saying once again, "It's nice to meet you, Miss Christina," which was all so obviously ridiculous that Erika turned around and looked at me like she was going to punch me in the nose.

Maybe I deserved it, but if you think about it, things were pretty stacked against me that day. First I go to a topless beach and am expected to have no reaction. Then I'm expected to be cool around the most elegant woman on the planet. A tall order. Anyway, it's not like Erika was so innocent. Introduce her to some sporty-but-brainy college kid who goes to Harvard and she can barely speak. Of course, one might say that it's more noble to be impressed with brains than with physical and social attributes. But I'm a complete academic disgrace. I failed every class that semester. So how did she think I felt when she got all excited by so-called educated people? It upsets me now just talking about it.

Anyway, Christina said, "Why don't you follow me?" and then led us back into a very large entryway. The house was per-fectly decorated—looked like something out of a museum—and there were huge paintings on the walls.

"Can I offer you something to drink?" she said as we fol-lowed her past a large, open living room.

"I'm okay," Erika said.

I thought about getting a scotch. Wanted to act cool. But I thought better of it and said that I was "okay too."

Christina then opened a door and led us into another room—kind of a second living room. It was very formal, very serious, and not at all beachy. In fact, it was kind of dark. The curtains were drawn, the couches were a kind of rich dark brown, and everything smelled like the high-end oil you use to treat exotic wood from the Amazon. It was a good place to have high-level meetings about murderers and international terrorists. Very private. Very secure. Very hard to get shot in the back of the head in a room like that.

Anyway, Christina told us that Lubchenko (or Anton, as she was calling him) knew we were there. "He'll be in shortly," she said, in her quiet, breathy English. "I'm afraid today has been very busy for him, though, so he might be a few minutes."

"Okay," I said.

"Are you sure you wouldn't like something to drink?" she asked again.

"I think we're fine," Erika said.

"All right," she said, smiling, and then she left the room.

I looked at Erika, and she looked back at me.

"This is quite a place, huh?" I said.

"It is quite a place," she replied.

We sat down and prepared to wait. But the wait wasn't long. In another minute, Lubchenko walked through the door.

30

E van, Erika," Lubchenko said as he shut the door behind him. "I have to say I'm a little surprised." He was talking in this kind of strange and serious tone. "But only that you are here. I think I have a sense of what you're looking for. But I'm surprised you found me."

Lubchenko was enormous. Not tall or fat. Just enormous, like everything was oversized on him. He had a huge barrel chest, thick muscular hands, a long hard jaw, and a heavy black mustache that it would take me ninety years to grow. And he looked a little healthier since the last time I saw him. Or, he looked tanned—like he had spent a lot of time working on his roses. All very impressive. No joke. Have to say that all I could think about that instant was that I was glad I was there. This guy was the real thing. If he couldn't help us, we had no chance. Really.

Anyway, I finally replied: "We found your address at Lubchenko Auto. And then the concierge at the building gave us a letter that came for you after you had left. It had a return address. This one."

"Interesting," Lubchenko said, nodding. "And I suppose you also read the letter?" Pause. I didn't know what to say.

Lubchenko finally continued, "Well, it doesn't matter." Another pause. "Now, I assume you're here because of Richmond and Switzerland."

"How much do you know about it?"

"I've been picking up chatter for a while. And I saw what happened on the news. In Seattle. Richmond is a very smart man—it's not easy to fool the authorities in this day and age."

"So you think he made it through with the virus?"

"Yes. He landed in Switzerland this morning. With the virus."

"It was us that called the police, you know."

"I wondered. But what did you know?"

"Nothing, really. We got an anonymous call a few days ago telling us that Richmond was going to be transporting the small-pox for sale in Switzerland."

Erika added, "And that he was going to kill the three of us and Evan's father after the deal went through."

"You didn't have someone make that call, did you?" I suddenly said.

Lubchenko laughed. "Why would I do that?"

"To protect us?"

"It wasn't me," he simply said. "I wasn't trying to protect you." He paused for a moment, and then continued. "But I think I can prevent Richmond from putting his plans into action."

Well, that at least was something solid. It was great news, in fact. I was happy.

But I was sitting in a chair that was definitely designed for style rather than comfort, and (because I have a hard time keeping my priorities straight) I suddenly realized that my back was aching. I had been sitting for too long, and now that we were talking about such heavy things, I suddenly felt a kind of shooting pain up my back. Extremely annoying. But I tried to concentrate, as difficult as that is for me. Had to concentrate. I leaned forward, watching Lubchenko consider everything. Finally he spoke again. "Well, we need to have some kind of plan. I've been thinking about it since I found out about Richmond's trip, and, indeed, I have a small operation in action right now. But I'm afraid I don't have all the information I need yet. I don't mean to offend you, but frankly, I'm a bit more worried about your father than I am about you. I'd prefer for him to stay alive for reasons that I can't really explain to you at this point."

That was kind of a surprising thing to hear. And then Lubchenko said something else that was fairly unexpected.

"I should tell you that I'm having troubles of my own within my group," he said. "The man you met at the Café Saint-Beauvais when we first met, my assistant, a man whose name is Rybakov, has turned against me, and I'm afraid that he knows quite a bit about me and my plans for the future."

"That guy at the Saint-Beauvais," Erika said. "He was so nice."

Lubchenko laughed. "Yes, in that setting, he's very nice. But I don't think you'd like him very much if you knew some of the things he's done."

"Probably not," Erika agreed.

There was a pause. Then Lubchenko started talking again. "Look, I think we have just a small bit of time at this point. Richmond has to be careful. He got through security and made it past the FBI. And maybe the FBI thinks they were misled by a crank caller, which I now understand was you. But just because Richmond was clean doesn't mean he's off scot-free. They'll be keeping an eye on him, although not with the same kind of authority, especially since he's now in Switzerland. But I promise you the Swiss authorities haven't let this drop."

Again, another pause. After a moment I said, "But we need to do something soon, right?"

Lubchenko hesitated, then said, "I need to think about all this. We can't afford any false moves. Richmond is too smart. What I need you to do at this point is wait for just a bit. I need to think. Is there a way I can reach you? At your hotel?"

"We have a cell phone," Erika said.

"Good, then you don't have to hide in your hotel room. You can see Saint-Tropez while I make some phone calls and come up with something. I'm afraid the plan might not include you. You might not see me again, in fact. But I'll call to let you know where we stand."

"But you're going to take care of this."

"Believe me, I want to take care of this more than you know. But I need the afternoon to make arrangements. So, perhaps we ought to conclude our meeting."

Lubchenko stood up, and Erika and I followed suit. As he turned, his sports coat opened slightly, and I could see the silvery handle of a gun resting below his shoulder. Chilling. But at least it wasn't pointed at me.

"It was good to see you," Lubchenko now said, opening the door and stepping out into the hall. "I'm sorry it was under these circumstances, however."

"We are too," I said.

Lubchenko then walked to the front door, with us following close behind. Christina was nowhere to be seen, but I didn't really mind. Too much to think about. Finally we got to the front door—it was a long hall—and Lubchenko opened it.

"I'll talk to you this evening," he said.

We stepped out onto the front path. The sudden smell of flowers and plants was strange. The smell didn't seem to match the conversation we were having.

"Okay," I said. "This evening."

Lubchenko smiled, turned, and headed back into his house, shutting the door behind him.

I looked at Erika as I started down the path to the car. "Always a mystery with this guy," I said.

"Always," she replied. "But what can we do? We've got to wait."

S o, we had to wait. Seemed like something
less of a plan than I expected. But on the
other hand, I didn't really have any idea what we
should do. And as we got into our car, back on
the street, it occurred to me that having
Lubchenko at work with us was actually pretty
comforting. It at least addressed two of the major
problems: (1) the matter of smallpox being sold to terrorists—
Lubchenko would obviously be much better than me at stopping this, and (2) he said he wanted to keep my father alive,
which was also something he'd be better at than me.

Sadly, he didn't make too big of a deal about keeping me,
Erika, and Ruben alive. I mean, I'm sure he didn't want to see
us dead. But again, this guy was ruthless, no matter what his
final intentions were, and I'm sure that if it was going to com-
promise him in any way, he'd let us die rather than jeopardize
his plans.

But I did figure he'd save us if it didn't make a difference
one way or another. And that was something. When the world
is about to be hit with a plague, and a bad guy wants to blow
your brains out, you take comfort where you can find it. *I just
have to stay alert,* I thought, and then I remembered that it was

about time to check in with Ruben. As I pulled onto the street, I clumsily opened the cell phone on my knee as I did a U-turn. And as we started back down the hill, I placed the call. (I am a very irresponsible driver, by the way.)

Anyway, the phone in the hotel room rang several times. And then several more.

More times than I was comfortable with, frankly. But finally Ruben answered.

"Ruben?" I said.

"Yep," he replied.

"Why so many rings?"

"I was in the bathroom. Leave me alone. What's up?"

"Just checking in. All's cool. We're on our way back."

"Great. Anything happen I should know about?"

"Well, we've got to wait around a bit. Lubchenko's going to think things over. But this was a good idea. We're a hundred times better off at this point. But I'll tell you about it when we get back. I think we should go to a restaurant because I'm absolutely starving. And thirsty."

"And then back to the beach?" Ruben said.

"You said you hate the beach, Ruben."

"I like it now. It's growing on me."

At this point, Erika jumped in. "We're not going back to the beach," she said. "Tell that to Ruben right now. It's like a fraternity house with you guys."

"You're in trouble," I told Ruben. "No beach."

"I knew it. Erika always spoils everything."

Anyway, eventually I hung up with Ruben, made a left turn, and got back on the main road that was going to take us back to the hotel—about a ten-minute trip. Frankly, I was glad we weren't going back to the beach again. Too much to think about—trying not to blush, trying not to say the wrong thing in front of Erika, trying to keep my eyes turned politely away. There's only so much a man can handle, and I had a lot on my plate at that exact moment.

32

S o I was pretty happy that we had the cell phone. At least we didn't have to stay cooped up in the hotel. This was good. I wanted to see more of the city. And as we walked into the hotel lobby, I marveled over my incredible ability to enjoy myself in any situation. In fact, I was so impressed, I even told Erika about it.

"You know what's great about me?" I said.

"What?" Erika replied, rolling her eyes.

"I can always have a good time, no matter what the situation."

"Uh-huh."

"I mean, dangerous plans are afoot, and here I am thinking about having a late lunch on the hotel's terrace."

"You're an amazing man, Evan Macalister."

"And then maybe a little shopping. Maybe I'll get some new shorts or some kind of hat."

"Your bravery is astounding."

"Don't worry, honey. I'm not going to forget you. I'll get you a hat as well."

"Great. A hat."

"You're a lucky woman."

"I certainly am."

"You certainly are."

"I think I'm getting my own room tonight, Evan, because, like, you're kind of driving me crazy."

As she said this, I stuck the key in the door and turned the knob. Time to grab Ruben and get some food.

Sadly, however, our plans changed. And rather quickly. Apparently, as I discovered when I opened the door, quite a bit had happened since he and I last talked. Quite a bit.

"Hi," Ruben said.

I wanted to say hi back, but I was totally speechless.

Ruben was sitting near the window, looking out onto the beach. And to his left, sitting on a small chair that belonged to the writing desk, was Lubchenko's former assistant from the Café Saint-Beauvais, pointing a fairly large gun with a silencer at Ruben's head.

So strange. Seemed like I had seen this exact scene before—just last spring, when Richmond's now dead lackey, Colburn, had *his* gun pointed at Ruben. I almost said something about all this. But the assistant (or "Rybakov," the guy Lubchenko now said was working against him) quickly started talking.

"Do as I say or your friend will be killed," he said. "Close the door and sit on the bed. Remember where my gun is pointed."

I was by the door, and I probably could have made a break for it—could have gone for help. But that would have been it for Ruben. These guys were always serious when they made threats. Instead I reached behind me, pushed the door closed, and sat down on the bed.

"What do you want?" I asked.

"I'm here on business," he replied. "I hear you went to see Anton. Or Lubchenko, as I know you like to call him. I'd say I was curious about what you said to him, but I'm sure I already know."

"I'm sure you know everything. So why are you here? Are you going to kill us?" I was trying to sound tough, but I think my scratchy, jittery voice gave me away. It's a hard thing to handle—thinking you're going to go hat shopping only to meet a guy waving a gun at you.

"It's possible," he said. "But probably somebody else will kill you. I'm afraid to say you've become a very important part of the deal I'm working on. That is to say, you've become part of the price. Your friend Jim Richmond won't give us what we want unless we deliver you to Switzerland."

I tried not to look surprised, but I could feel my skin turning red. Funny—even with all we knew about Richmond, it was still shocking to hear that he was now targeting us in this whole deal. I mean, as creeped out as Richmond made me feel, part of me was always trying to give him the benefit of the doubt.

"So you're taking us to Switzerland?" I asked.

"Yes, I'm taking you to Switzerland," he replied. "To Geneva." Suddenly there was a knock at the door. Rybakov very casually stood up and asked, through the door, who it was.

"Ilya," a voice from behind the door called out.

"Well, this is all right on schedule," Rybakov said, opening the door. In walked a very large man in a suit (have to assume this was Ilya), followed by two other guys. They were well dressed and kind of handsome and refined looking. Didn't look like total thugs. But they had pretty mean looks in their eyes. Or pretty serious looks. Not the kind of dudes who were going to offer three kids too much pity. Too bad. Pity can get you a lot in this world.

"We're going to the airport," Rybakov said to us as the last goon shut the door. "We have a plane waiting. But first we're going to a limousine to take us there. We have a simple way of doing this. Evan first. Ruben and Erika will wait here until you're in the limo. Then they'll follow. If anyone does anything stupid, one of my men will call me on the cell phone, and his or her friends will be shot in the face. We'll do it without thinking twice. And we'll get away with it. I promise you that. So you're really best off doing exactly as we say."

"Okay," I said, after a pause. Erika and Ruben said the same.

What else were we going to say?

Anyway, pretty chilling. I went first, leaving the room with Rybakov still pointing his gun at Ruben.

I do have to say that I still thought about doing something as I walked through the hotel lobby with two bad guys behind me. They obviously didn't have their guns drawn. And there were people everywhere. I could definitely escape. But at the cost of Ruben's and Erika's lives. Anyway, quite wisely, I thought better of escaping. I just kept my mouth shut, walked out of the hotel, and got into the limo.

What a hero.

And now the gun was pointed at me. By a big guy with bad teeth who was smiling at me. We were in a fully armored, black-windowed limo. One of these guys could shoot me with a gun and a silencer without a single drunken tourist knowing anything. No wonder he was smiling. I (on the other hand) was pretty freaked out, as you might imagine. I mean, what if Ruben and Erika tried to make a break for it? I'd be splattered all over the limo's super-soft, high-end leather interior. What a way to go.

But after a few minutes, the door opened, and Erika, Ruben, Rybakov, and the other goon appeared and got in the car. Good that they hadn't flipped out. I was alive for the time being. But now we were speeding off to the airport, on our way to Geneva.

33

So just to give you a sense of time, we got back from Lubchenko's at about two o'clock. By two twenty, we were sitting in the cramped hotel room with a gun pointed at us. By two thirty, we were in the limo, headed to a small airport just outside Saint-Tropez.

"It's so nice here," I said, looking out the windows. "I'm a bit upset that you guys didn't give us more of a chance to see it."

"You have bigger worries than tourism," Rybakov said.

And this was true. Still, that's how I deal with worries. I make sarcastic remarks and wildly inappropriate jokes. This is something that school officials, my father, and everyone else who yelled at me didn't quite understand. I know that I don't take things as seriously as I should, that I'm a scatterbrain, that I'm a pain in the ass, etc., etc., etc. But when I'm really frightened, or feeling extremely pathetic, or feel like I've somehow disappointed everybody, I can't help it. In fact, my personality (which is normally so lovable and charming) just becomes more intense, extreme, exaggerated. That is, I become even more sarcastic. This is why I was always in detention. I could never resist that last smart-ass remark. I don't know. Maybe it's one of the things a human being has to learn—how to keep certain tendencies in check. But I never learned it.

"No, I want you to know that I'm really upset," I replied. "I really like it here. They have topless beaches. And palm trees. And we have a hotel room. And we've even rented a car—a car that is parked at a meter on the street, by the way. So I'm upset with you for doing this to us. You personally."

Rybakov just smiled and looked away. Again, strange that I've always stuck to these personality traits, even though they've gotten me nowhere over the years. But it was starting to make people nervous. "All right, Evan," Ruben said (calmly and without anger). "Let's keep our cool."

Erika put her hand on mine. Strange, but I couldn't figure out if she was telling me to shut up or trying to comfort me. The fact is that Erika knew me pretty well, and she could tell when I was scared, and as I thought about all this, my sarcastic position suddenly softened just a bit and I thought how lucky I was to be going out with her. I mean it. I was really lucky. This person who knew me so well, and let me be a wise-ass, and who teased me back just as hard, but seemed to like me so much. Whatever. That's one of the things about moments of terror— the wide range of emotions you feel. You feel tough, then you feel scared, then you feel love, and then you move on to the next emotion. I looked over at Erika and could tell she was stumbling along in the same way. Just minutes earlier, she had this calm, defiant look on her face. Now she was looking like she might start to cry. And that look was pretty upsetting. I suddenly felt very, very bad that she was involved in all this. No way she deserved to have guns in her face. It was a very troubling thought. And it didn't really go away.

Still, after about twenty minutes, we were at the next leg of our journey, and new distractions arose.

"We're here," Rybakov said. "Again, I advise you to do exactly what we say."

We passed through these large metal gates at the edge of the airport grounds, and after making our way past a few buildings, we drove out onto the tarmac and right up to a very expensive-looking, double-engine private jet with a pilot in uniform standing by stairs that dipped down to the ground.

"Is this for us?" Erika asked as we came to a halt.

"This is for us," Rybakov replied, reaching over her and opening the door. "Just get out and walk right up those stairs. As you can see, there's nowhere for you to run."

We slowly stepped out of the limo. I think each of us was looking for some way out, but there wasn't one. We would have been shot before we made it five feet. Ruben looked at me and flashed me a look that said something along the lines of, *What the hell are we going to do now?*

Sadly, I was flashing him the same look back.

Anyway, we got on the plane. And again, for the sake of the timeline, I'll add that it was now ten minutes to three.

34

So when you're in a private plane with four guys who tell you that they're going to kill you, it gives you time to think. I thought about what an idiot I was. And I don't mean a funny idiot—the Evan Macalister who's loads of fun to be around at parties. I mean a stupid idiot. The guy who steals computer equipment, gets involved in international terrorist plots, gets nabbed by bad guys, and ensures that he, his friends, and his father all get shot.

The worst thing about all this was that there seemed to be no way out. I mean, before, we always had a backup plan: go to the police, spill our guts, and take whatever punishment they dished out. It didn't seem like we were going to have much of an opportunity to get to the cops this time around.

And I felt guilt. I mean, I was pretty much the source of everyone's despair and misery. Sure, I saved my dad from jail the last time around. And I was doing my best to prevent an international biological catastrophe. But the bottom line was that we were all on a plane, we were headed to Switzerland, we were going to get shot, smallpox virus was going to get sold, and then my dad was going to get whacked. A pretty unsuccessful mission, if you think about it.

But don't get me wrong. I may have been pretty philosophical at that moment, but I was also scared out of my wits. I mean, sure, I felt guilt. But I also didn't really want to die. I had a full life ahead of me. There were lots of fun things I planned to do. Seemed pretty unfair that these freaks in black suits were going to put an end to all that. And, to be quite honest, it seemed grossly unfair that I'd had to spend so much of my life taking classes at Pencrest. Nothing like impending death to make you feel like you've wasted your life "learning" things.

But let me tell you something else I thought about. I actually thought about a million things. It's amazing the kind of thought density that occurs in moments of great stress. I mean, my mind was racing. But there was one thing I kept thinking about—a thing that actually was more relevant than most of the things that were passing through my mind.

So when my dad started the company, he was way leveraged. That means he was way in debt—that's how he got the company started. He went to banks. He went to private investors. He even set it up that he owed his employees money. And he worked with Richmond, who had money of his own and (to be absolutely honest) was a highly qualified research doctor. The point is that we weren't always rich. I mean, my father always did well. He was a doctor, after all. But he was no millionaire.

Anyway, that changed. He made some good decisions about an arthritis drug. He backed an allergy medication that's used in a lot of hospitals. And he developed the cancer drug that eventually made MRI what it was. And so, one day, almost overnight really, we were rich. Really rich.

Now, as you know, my father is a frugal guy. Hates to spend money. But my mom wasn't like that. Again, she was a doctor too, so she had plenty of her own money. And she liked to blow it on me—or on the family. I mean, she was pretty careful. She didn't buy a lot of stupid crap. But she did things to make life more fun. Like, she gave me an allowance—a thing my dad never did—and she'd take us on vacations, etc. But when the millions started rolling in, she decided that we needed a beach house, and she started looking.

Now, my dad is genetically wired to hate things like beach houses. Nothing could be more ridiculous or wasteful in his eyes. He despised all forms of leisure and worked most of his life to make the world less fun for those around him. But he loved my mom. That's a fact. She was pretty much the one thing that brought any kind of joy into his life, besides work (if you can call that kind of thing joy). So my mother got what she wanted. My dad didn't want a beach house. But he wanted my mother to be happy. So when he started making it big, and started making millions of dollars, she headed to the Pacific coast, to a beach town called Wyndham (about two hours away from Seattle), and bought this beautiful gray-shingled house that sat right on top of a rocky outcropping overlooking the ocean. It was a beautiful place. It really was. And while I can't say with any sense of accuracy that my dad liked it, I will say that it relaxed him, although I think this is because it made my mother so happy, which, again, was one of the only things my dad really cared about.

Anyway, that first stretch of time there (late spring) was pretty great. I was eleven, and my mom had long ago taken time off from her career as a medical scientist to raise me—I was an enormous handful, after all—so we split together for the beach for weekends during the end of the school year and then, when school was out, for the whole summer. My dad would even come down on weekends, although he had a pretty nice study at the house and still spent a lot of time working. But it was really happy. We were all happy. Even my dad. Incredible. Imagine. A happy man. Now, two points on all this.

First, Mr. Richmond came down one weekend in early May. We planned to do a lot of entertaining at the house that spring and summer, although I've got to say things that particular weekend seemed pretty strained. There was no trouble. Nothing overt or obvious. But it was a strange weekend. It was unusually warm for May, so we went to the beach. And we played tennis at the local courts, went out to eat in Wyndham, and did a bunch of other things. And my mother cooked crabs and steak on Saturday night, which we ate on the deck that overlooked the ocean. But it was weird. I'd never really seen the three of them interact like that before—on a purely social level for an extended period of time. I was eleven, so I wasn't really too keyed in on the "social dynamics of adults," as they say. But it seemed strained.

But maybe it seemed this way to me because of a pretty strange thing that happened that Saturday afternoon. We had gone to the beach (which was a short walk down a rocky pathway along the cliff that our house sat on) and set up our beach chairs, cooler, etc., on a patch near where the waves always broke closest to the shore. It really was a short walk, though. Again, our house was on the ocean (although we were up on the cliff), so it took about five minutes to get back to the house. And after we had all settled in (my mother with a novel, my dad with stacks of boring medical journals), Mr. Richmond got up and said he needed to run back to the house for something. He was gone for some time, and during this time I had to pee—something I did (and do) quite frequently. Drove my father nuts. Just like Ruben drove me nuts. Anyway, I headed back up to the house and was walking around upstairs, headed to the bathroom nearest my bedroom, when I spotted Mr. Richmond in my parents' room going through my mother and father's dresser. He was just in the top drawer. Couldn't imagine that there was anything in there he'd want. Still can't. But it was very, very strange.

Anyway, I was kind of surprised and didn't know what was going on, so I just stood there and watched for a few minutes until finally he looked up and saw me. He was shocked at first.

Kind of jumped a little bit. But then he smiled—that studied Richmond smile that he flashes—and said, "Heya, sport, how's it going?"

I didn't know what to say. I didn't think he was doing anything wrong, really. I was a kid. What did I know? But I knew it was a little weird.

"I needed something of your dad's for work," he said. "Office stuff. We share all sorts of things. But you know what, I've got to admit that I should have asked first. It was just that I didn't want to go all the way back to the beach because I knew he'd say yes. I knew he'd tell me to go ahead and get it. But I should have asked. So what do you say we keep this a secret? Too much explaining to do. And you know your dad. You know how he gets."

Again, I was kind of young. But I knew it was strange. But I also still had a certain kind of faith in adults. So what was I going to do?

"Okay," I said. And then I found my way to the bathroom.

Truthfully, I didn't think too much of it after that. Not with any kind of real attention, at any rate. But I didn't forget it either. Always kind of puzzled me. Still, didn't think about it too much. I'd say I don't know why, but I guess it's because there were plenty of other things on my mind that summer. Or, one fairly large thing.

In the second week of June, in the middle of this stretch of beautiful weather that's still famous down in Wyndham, my mom got the flu. Or we thought it was the flu. It was a fever. A pretty bad one. And while fevers are pretty normal, this one didn't go away. She had a temperature of about 103 for about five days before my dad insisted she go to the hospital. She didn't want to. She said it would pass. It was just the flu. But my dad insisted. She went to Briggs County Hospital (the county where Wyndham was), and she stayed there for three days. They couldn't really find anything wrong with her, so they said it was probably just some weird virus. Frankly, it's what any hospital would have said. It's what my dad said. And I'm sure it's what he thought. But after three days of her not getting better, he said we were moving my mother. To a hospital in Seattle. And we quickly packed up and headed for the city, where my mother continued to stay in the hospital, still with a terrible fever, still hooked up to an IV, but still with no word on what was going on. But then they did an MRI—a kind of high-end X-ray—and found something that seemed strange. A spot on her liver. A small one, really. Not anything that any normal person would think twice about, if a normal person were looking over X-rays, that is. But it worried the doctors. And it worried my father. So they opened her up to take a look at it. And one night in late June, my father came into my bedroom and told me that my mother had cancer, and that it was very, very serious. I was old enough to know what that meant, so there was no sugar coating this. And I knew how sick my mom had been with that weird fever. Still, my dad tried to reassure me. He said that my mother had a chance to pull through. "She's got a shot at making it," he said. "She's a tough one. But it's serious." One of my father's virtues is that he's no liar. I was getting the straight scoop. So I knew what "a shot" meant. "A shot" meant the odds were probably against her. And it turned out that even "a shot" was probably optimistic. By late July my mother was in a coma. And on the tenth of August, she died. It was incredibly rapid, even for cancer. But it's an unpredictable disease, and the doctors couldn't stop it.

Anyway, we never went back to the house. My dad sold it in September, and as much as I loved the place, I was glad. My dad did his best to keep things as normal as possible, but he wasn't a fool. He didn't make us do foolish things to pretend like nothing had happened. So the beach house was over. We weren't going back.

But it is funny, what you think about when you're frightened. Like I said, I must have had a million other thoughts on that plane ride.

Like, here's something else I thought. It was pretty clear that we were headed to Switzerland to be delivered to Richmond. Rybakov said as much. And it's pretty clear that Richmond wasn't looking for us just to make sure we got back safely to Seattle. But for whatever a madman that guy was, I still held out some kind of hope for him. Or I still thought that he wouldn't hurt us. That he couldn't hurt us. That he wouldn't be capable of it. I mean, the guy was definitely freaky and slimy. But freaky and slimy is a far cry from a guy who'll put a bullet in your head. Strange, though. It was dead clear that we were a threat to him and that he'd have to get us out of the way. But I just had this kind of hope. Or, I just still wasn't able to believe it.

Whatever. When you're trapped in a plane with a bunch of guys with guns, you hold on to whatever you can. You have crazy ideas that your enemy will somehow spare your life. And it's not that implausible. It's a hard thing to imagine—someone wanting to kill you. But it's only hard to imagine because human beings are very naive when it comes to this kind of thing.

A nyway. The story.
    We landed at about five twenty. That part
was over. We arrived at a big airport, but we
were on the side where the private planes
landed, and we were able to taxi over to another
limousine that was waiting for us.

"Time to get off," Rybakov said. "We'll be seeing your friend Mr. Richmond soon. Again, I want to remind
you that you can't escape. And if you try, we'll kill you. We
won't think twice."

The way he said it was so matter-of-fact that you knew he
was serious. No wild threats from this guy. Just the facts—a list
of actions and consequences—and that's all.

Anyway, needless to say, Ruben, Erika, and I did what we
were told. And in a few minutes, we were back in another huge
limousine, speeding into Geneva, bypassing all the mess that
you normally have to go through (passports, customs, etc.)
because when your escorts are highly connected bad guys, no
one seems to bother you.

It wasn't exactly clear where we were going at first, but we
soon pulled up in front of another hotel. Initially I was a bit surprised—thought we'd be at someone's hilltop mansion. But we

were headed to meet Richmond, who, although he was something of a business partner, was also on the other side of the
trade. That is, Rybakov and he may have been making a deal,
but that was no reason to go and trust someone. You want to
be somewhere neutral like a hotel for that kind of thing—not in
a place like someone's ski chalet, which could be a serious trap.
(See how much I know about how to execute evil plans?
Amazing really.)

Anyway, this hotel was the perfect destination for bad guy
stuff. Quite a bit different from l'Archange in Saint-Tropez. This
hotel (called l'Etoile) was no tourist destination. No drunk people in tuxedos and slinky black dresses wandering in and out.
No bathing suits either. Just very serious businessmen in dark
suits, minding their own business, avoiding eye contact, and (I
imagine) thinking about money. Seemed to be a hotel designed
entirely for arms dealers and drug kingpins. Don't get me
wrong. This place was nice. Probably one of the nicest places
I've ever been. But there wasn't a lot of fanfare and gold trim.
Just cold marble, silent bellhops, and huge and incomprehensible pieces of abstract art.

"I don't think I'm going to like it here," I told one of the
goons as we walked past an enormous painting that consisted
of black and gray circles.

"You won't," he said. And he wasn't smiling.

Anyway, we walked past the front desk and onto a waiting
elevator without anyone so much as looking up at us. The deal

was the same. If I made a fuss, Erika and Ruben would be shot. But this was not the kind of place where making a fuss was even going to do much good. If I'd gone running to the hotel manager screaming bloody murder, he probably would have told me to stop making such a scene and die with a little dignity. Anyway, not good.

The suite we went to was on the top floor, at the end of a long hallway. It was pretty out of the way. No one was going to hear us calling for help up there. And it was huge inside. More like an apartment than anything else. Huge fireplace, lots of couches, a broad dining-room-sized table, and an expansive wet bar. Definitely the kind of place you'd want to get to impress clients (or trade smallpox vaccine, or kill three innocent young people). There was also a huge row of windows that covered the entire back wall. But the curtains were drawn, so no one was going to see anything through them. And there were two doors in the back—clearly a couple of bedrooms off the main living area. Anyway, big and private. Not much more to say.

"Get comfortable," Rybakov said after we had all finally arrived.

"Comfortable," Ruben groaned. "I'm afraid that's not very likely."

"Jim Richmond will be here shortly," Rybakov continued as the three of us sat on one of the pieces of the large sectional couch. "He'll be very happy to see you."

"And we'll be happy to see him," I replied. Another sarcastic remark. But I've got to say that at this point, wising off wasn't making me feel any better. I was pretty much as scared as I've ever been.

So we waited. And it was pretty agonizing. And strange. A strange set of psychological problems came all at once—too quick to keep track of. Like, there was a very strong chance I was going to die. So, that was on my mind. A little distraction, as they say. But I was also thinking about what it would be like to see Richmond.

Again, despite the fact that I had once suspected he was in on all this, and despite the fact that I always found him to be a bit slimy, I still couldn't get my mind around it. I still couldn't quite understand the full implications of all this. And I just didn't know what it would be like to see him. Now that everything was out in the open. What would he say to me?

It was a puzzle. A heavy one. But it was solved soon enough.

About fifteen minutes after we arrived, there was a knock on the door. One of the bodyguard guys stepped up to the little peephole in the door. In another second, he was turning the knob. Three new guys in dark suits stepped forward. And behind them stepped Richmond.

He had a kind of matter-of-fact look on his face, and the first thing he did was step up to Rybakov and shake his hand.

"Everything on track?" Richmond said.

"Everything," Rybakov said.

At this point, Richmond turned and looked at me and very calmly said, "How's it going, champ? They treating you all right?"

I opened my mouth to respond, but nothing came out. I was literally speechless. What could I say to that? It was strange. It was exactly the same kind of thing that always came out of his mouth. Not one bit different—not the words, not the tone, not the emphasis. He was totally calm. And while calmness in this kind of situation can sometimes be good, that was not the case here. Was this guy really such a psychopath? A guy so incapable of empathy? I mean, was all this just something he was doing for laughs? Completely mind-boggling.

But I did manage to speak. I did manage to say something.

I said, "Yeah. Fine."

That showed him. Really denounced him as the evil criminal he was.

He just smiled and said, "Good. Good. I'm glad to hear it." Then he opened his cell phone and started typing in numbers as he walked to the back of the room. In another second, he opened a door to one of the bedrooms and then disappeared.

Strangely, I felt a sudden sort of relief. I was definitely no safer. But just looking at him sent chills down my spine.

But the door opened suddenly again, and Richmond stepped back out. He looked at me from across the room and

said, in a very controlled way (almost as though he was psych-
ing himself up for something or playing a part he wasn't quite
sure he was ready for), "You know I'm going to have to kill you,
right, Evan?"

Again, speechless. How do you respond to something like
that? Even I couldn't come up with a response, and I can never
keep my mouth shut. Richmond just looked straight at me for a
moment. Then he looked back down at his cell phone, hit
another button, and disappeared back into the room.

S o there you go. Any doubts had now been addressed. Of course, you might argue that saying you'll do something and doing it are two different things. But in this situation, I'd say they were pretty close. Another bad guy might have wanted the killing done out of the way, without having to "dirty his own hands." But I'd say that Richmond was now getting ready to be in on the dirty work.

And another fact became pretty clear to me as well. There was a virtual army of bad guys in the room. Richmond, Rybakov, and six goons in all. So, eight armed guys who had clearly all killed before. Any possibility of us fighting our way out was looking pretty slight. Even with a man as tough as me.

Ruben and Erika seemed to be having the same grim thoughts.

"We're dead," Ruben kept mumbling under his breath. Normally this was the kind of thing he yelled—or squealed, really. But this time the words were soft. This time he wasn't just panicking but stating a pretty clear fact. The writing was on the wall, as it were, and Ruben was softly reading it to himself.

Erika, too, looked pretty bad. She wasn't mumbling to herself. But she looked pretty white, pretty peaked. Even her lips had a kind of ashen color. She was sitting next to me and gently squeezing my hand. Not in a very reassuring way, though.

Still, have to say that I managed to maintain at least a glimmer of hope. I mean, don't get me wrong. I was completely freaked out too. I was definitely as scared as Ruben and Erika. But (in general) I'm a fairly delusional guy. And I couldn't help but hold out a little hope for something. Lubchenko knew what was going on. And maybe my father had some inkling that bad things were afoot. Long shots. And at this point, highly improbable. But again, I'm not a very quick-witted guy when it comes to this stuff. Again, delusional.

Anyway, in about five minutes, Richmond came out of the room again. He was silent and looked thoughtful as Ruben, Erika, and I looked up at him. I did not want to face him. Did not want to talk to him again. And I suddenly had this sick feeling like I was going to vomit if he looked at me again or called me something like "tiger" or "big guy." But just as he approached the center of the room, there was another knock on the door.

"The deal begins," Richmond said, looking over at me and smiling. Then he pointed at the door, and one of his lackeys went and opened it.

Now, let me just say that I can maintain my optimistic delusions through thick and thin. Almost nothing makes me feel like all is completely lost. This, for instance, is how I can go to test after test in school without having studied one bit and still think that I'm going to pass—or even somehow pull something as unlikely as a C or a B. That said, what happened next pretty much put an end to my vague idea that there still might be some way out.

The door opened. There was a moment of hesitation. I couldn't quite see what was going on. Was a very confusing scene. And then it became more unexplainable. Was frankly shocking—I was even more blown away than when Richmond arrived. In through the door walked Lubchenko—serious look on his face and ready to do business. And behind him was a new guy in a suit who carried two very expensive- and very secure-looking briefcases.

Still, I couldn't understand what was going on. I really couldn't. I mean, it should have been very clear what I was now up against. But I couldn't understand what had happened. I almost felt glad, like Lubchenko had arrived and now I'd be saved. Then Lubchenko passed us (without looking over) and, in a very masculine and robust way, embraced Rybakov (as European men sometimes do).

And then he turned and did the same thing to Richmond. Hugged him. Old friends. Comrades. Brothers in arms. "Do you have the money?" Richmond said with a kind of sick look on his face.

"It's in the briefcases. Let's count it."

And then as they hugged, and then as they talked about the money, I finally understood. I should have before. But it really took that hug to do it. Lubchenko was in on the deal. He was one of them. He was a bad guy. He was the one buying the smallpox virus. And again, my idiocy was confirmed.

"You liar," I finally blurted out. "You totally lied to us."

I've got to say that Lubchenko had the air of a very powerful mob boss. You really wanted him to like you, really wanted him to be your friend. And when he was your friend, he had this sort of gentle and protective powerfulness that made you feel very safe. But when it turned against you, it was terrifying. As I found out. Lubchenko quickly turned to me and Erika and Ruben and snapped, "The three of you have been very stupid getting involved in things you know nothing about. And now you're going to pay for it."

I can't quite describe how this made me feel. It wasn't so much what he said as the deliberate and final tone that he delivered it with. Nothing like Richmond, who always revealed himself as a kind of greedy coward, even when he was just bragging about buying a ski chalet. Lubchenko was the real thing. He was driven by deeper things than greed, and I've got to say that for the first time that day (even with all that had happened), I felt like bursting into tears. It was like getting yelled at by a coach or a friend's parents who you really liked, who you really wanted to like you. It was a terrible, terrible feeling. It made no sense. I should have felt hatred and deep anger. I guess I did. I felt those things. But mostly I felt deeply betrayed. And it was terrible. So terrible that it almost crowded out the other sudden feeling that I had—the feeling that my delusional optimism had finally given way and this was really it, this was really where my life was going to end.

This is a fact that I've discovered: when a man faces death, he thinks about love. I'd had a gun in my face twice in my life by that point, and both times the thoughts were the same. You don't feel anger. You don't even feel that scared. You think about the people you care about and who care about you, and you think about how you love them.

As Lubchenko and Richmond walked to the back of the room, I looked at Erika and Ruben and thought about how I loved these guys, and how they loved me, and how lucky I was to have such good friends (even as profoundly *unlucky* as I felt at that moment). And I think they were thinking the same thing. Erika looked at me and said, "I'm glad I'm with you. I'm glad I'm not alone." And then she turned to Ruben and said the same thing. And then Ruben looked back at us and said, "I love you guys," which under other circumstances would make me want to retch but here seemed to make perfect sense. And I said I loved them, and Erika said she loved us, and we all held hands because what the hell else were we going to do?

But my mind was also in other places. Amazing how quickly you can think in a situation like this, but I'll tell you that one of the things you really think about is your mother. It's cliché.

38

Almost embarrassing, really. But you really do. You think about your mother, and how she loved you, and how you loved her, and how much pain it would probably cause her if she knew what was happening to you. My mother was dead. So there'd be no tears from her when my body was found at the bottom of some alpine lake in Switzerland. But just the thought of it all—of her giving birth to a son that wasn't going to make it to his seventeenth birthday—seemed deeply sad to me.

Strange, but one of the ways that you can tell if you love someone is by how you feel when you watch them suffer. I hate to say this, but it's true. I'll tell you this because it's important in a larger cosmic way and because it's important in a way that's specifically relevant to the story. When my mother died of cancer, the hardest thing was watching her suffer. I thought about all the things that I was going to miss out on. I thought about how much I was going to miss her— when it was clear that she was going to die. But watching someone else suffer—watching them struggle to catch their breath, watching them talk about the things they're going to miss—that's as painful a thing as there is. And my mother was pretty brave; she didn't spend a lot of time complaining.

And let me say this. On a formal and official level, I deny categorically that I've ever felt anything close to what someone might call "love" for my father. I deny it. But since I'm being frank, up close, and personal, let me say that I knew I loved my father because of the way I felt when I saw him suffering over my mother's death. My dad's a hard-ass. More than that (and again), he acts out of a very deep sense of duty. So, there weren't too many tears shed in front of me. But as tough a guy as my dad was—and he's really the toughest guy I've ever met—I could still tell. I could still tell how much pain he felt. Long days when he said absolutely nothing. Sitting up all night alone in his study. And the rare and hidden tears—the kind of luxury that my father almost never allowed himself.

And then I thought about my father finding out that I was dead—and I realized how much pain it would cause him. I almost hoped Richmond got to him before he heard the news. As hard as my dad was on me, I had this image of him suddenly feeling very, very alone in the world—with my mother and me gone—and it kind of broke my heart.

Anyway, this is what I thought about. As I sat there holding Erika's hand, and as she held mine and Ruben's, and as Lubchenko and Richmond stood at the huge table at the far end of the room counting out the money, this is what I thought about.

But I have to say one more thing. A technical detail. You'll need to know it. As I've said, my mother died of cancer. But she died only after several rapid and drastic rounds of treatment. My father's company, MRI, made cancer-curing drugs, and, as I've also said at one time or another, the great tragedy of my mother's death is that she died of a cancer that my father's drugs had helped so many people overcome. This is important for you to know.

T hey spent about ten minutes counting the money. Richmond was a thorough guy. Wasn't going to let so much as a twenty go uncounted. I didn't have the greatest view of the scene, but every so often I'd see Richmond lift up a packet of what was clearly money—although not all of it American. Anyway, I don't know how much it was, but it had to be millions. A lot of millions. I know this mostly because of the way Richmond's eyes looked. He was like a kid with his hands stuck in a big jar of candy. He couldn't believe his luck and didn't want to pull his hands away. And Richmond was wealthy—it took a lot of money to get him going like that. But finally he had to pry himself away. They were on a schedule, after all. Couldn't stand there forever rubbing five-hundred-euro notes in their hands.

39

"Satisfied?" Lubchenko finally asked.

"Satisfied," Richmond replied. He pulled out his cell phone and in a few seconds started talking. "This is Richmond," he said. "We're good. Bring it in."

He closed the briefcases with the money and handed them to one of his crew. Then he walked into the middle of the room and looked at me. It was pretty horrifying, but I could tell he was still trying to psych himself up. Like, what was about to happen next was both something he wanted, and something that was hard for him to face. Still, he wasn't backing down. He paused for a moment, tilted his head down slightly, smiled a bit, then forced out, "It's not all about the money. It's really not."

Was he expecting a response from me? I don't know. But he didn't wait too long for me to say something. He just kept talking. "Do you know that I slept with your mother?" he said. "A long time ago. Before she met your father. In fact, I'm the one who introduced her to your father. I bet you never knew that."

I didn't know what to say, but I can tell you I suddenly felt extremely sick. "You're lying," I said quietly, almost trying to convince myself of it. I did know that Richmond introduced them. Anything else was news. But just the thought made me totally sick.

Richmond said, "I'm not lying, big guy," still seeming to force his way through the words. "She didn't like me, though. She liked me a little. She slept with me, after all. But it didn't last. And then she started going out with your father. After a company party. And that's when I knew what a little whore she was."

And that was enough for me.

I suddenly stood and lunged toward him, yelling, "You're a liar." But before I understood what was happening, I felt an enormous body fall on me from behind, and in the next instant

I was on the ground with one of the bodyguard guys on top of me. Painful. But I was too pissed to really care.

"Tie them up," Richmond said. "It's going to get a little rough, and I don't want them running around."

In the next second, the goons were tying us up. We struggled. Erika even turned and punched a guy in the face. Split his lip. Called him a "coward" and a "pig." But these guys were pretty big. And there were a lot of them. So even with us resisting, there wasn't much we could do. Once our wrists and legs were tied together, they propped us back up on the couch.

I was still furious. I guess that goes without saying. And the burning anger was total agony because I couldn't do a thing about it. But all I eventually said (or all that was intelligible) was, "I can't believe you're doing this to us. How could you? How long have you known me?"

Pathetic. I know. But I've got to say, as crazy as it sounds, even after everything that had happened, I still thought there might be some tiny part of Richmond that I could appeal to. But that changed. There I was, sitting there with my hands bound and entirely defenseless, when Richmond turned and punched me right in the mouth.

"That's enough," he said. He looked kind of stunned by the punch. Again, Richmond wanted to be a badass, but it was pretty clear that all this was still kind of jarring to him.

I was getting ready to start screaming again when there was another knock on the door.

"Here we go," Richmond said. Then he looked at me, forced a smile, and said, "Don't worry, tiger, it'll all be over soon enough."

One of Richmond's bodyguards opened the door, and in came two more guys in suits. One of them was carrying a black metal briefcase. He handed it to Richmond, who then took it back to where Lubchenko and Rybakov were.

"Open it and let's get through this," Lubchenko said. He looked over at me for a moment, and I've got to say that his blank stare was chilling. It was totally inscrutable, and I could only conclude that whatever was going on in his brain was extremely, extremely dark.

Richmond dialed in the combination lock on the briefcase, and in another second, the top popped open. Lubchenko paused for a moment and then stuck his hands into the briefcase. In the next moment he was staring at something in the palm of his hand. He smiled and walked back to the center of the room, to where we were sitting.

"Look at this, Evan," he said. "All this over such tiny little things." He held his hand out to me and I saw three pieces of what looked like clear plastic, with a tiny bit of liquid in them. "A man could destroy most of the world with this."

"I can't believe you're doing this," I said, again wondering if there was some way to reason with these guys. But he turned around as though he didn't even hear me and walked back to the table. He put the clear pieces of plastic back into the briefcase (which apparently had some kind of thick padding in it) and then looked up at Richmond.

"So, I suppose we should bring this to a conclusion," Lubchenko said. "Perhaps you'd like to do the honors, seeing that you know them best."

As he said this, he reached into his jacket and pulled out the silvery gun that I had seen earlier in Saint-Tropez. He then handed it to Richmond.

Strange, but at that moment, that afternoon in Saint-Tropez seemed like a million years away. Just that morning I had been standing slack-jawed and embarrassed on a topless beach, and now I was about to die. It's hard to explain, but the irony of it all was what was most on my mind. *It's just so strange,* I kept thinking. Maybe it was the way my mind was dealing with the larger, more complex questions that, of course, there were no answers for. Trying to piece together the events of the day was a more manageable problem than trying to figure out what happens when we die. And then I looked at Ruben, and then at Erika, and suddenly felt very, very scared. They were scared too. Ruben was crying. That was pretty rough to see. And Erika didn't look any better. And there wasn't much we could do to comfort one another. They looked at me. I looked at them. But what could we do? We were tied up, and these were bad dudes. This was the end.

But all that thinking passed in a brief instant. We didn't really have too long to think about it all. In the next second,

Richmond was walking toward me with this quick, unnatural, forced gait, like he was really having to work to psych himself up for this. And again, he looked scared. Really scared. Like this violence wasn't something he was used to or good at. But in the same look, I saw that he was going to go through with it. It might take some effort, but he was going through with it.

And then he said the following: "You know, I'm killing your father tonight too. Or I'm having him killed. In Brussels."

Richmond still looked like he was desperately struggling to get up the guts to go through with this, although the gun was now raised and pointed at me.

"The irony is endless," he said, "because, you know, I also helped to kill your mother."

This, I did not expect. Not in a million years. I didn't even know what he meant. But it was pretty jarring. Almost more jarring than having a gun to my head. My mother died of cancer. What the hell did he mean?

He just kept going, kept trying to work himself up to the thing that he was about to do. "She was sick already," he said, "so who knows what would have happened to her? But she was a whore. I told you that. So when they were treating her cancer with chemo that MRI produced, I made sure she had a bad batch. Not too bad. Just diluted. Basically, what was supposedly medicine was really mostly water. Blue water put in an IV bag and pumped into your mother. Not much of a cure. And now I'm going to kill you too."

And with that, he raised the gun to my head, and before I could respond, or even comprehend what he had just said to me, he pulled the trigger.

But there was only a clicking noise.

And then he pulled it again.

But again, there was only a clicking noise.

And then the guns in the room started blazing. Cracks from the guns with the silencers—deadly sounding but muffled. A truly, truly terrifying sound, especially as the blood started spattering on the furniture and the walls and the carpet and on me and Ruben and Erika. I have to say that I've never been that terrified. But I was most aware of how painless it all was. *This is painless,* I kept thinking, *I'm dying and it's painless,* although I couldn't figure out why. It was just so deeply confusing.

And then I breathed.

Deeply.

I had been holding my breath, and suddenly I started gulping in oxygen. And then I looked around, still trying to make sense of the scene. And then, before me, the picture became clearer. Richmond was dead—shot about five times. So were his men. And when I looked up, there was Lubchenko, and Rybakov, and their three henchmen, standing with guns drawn over the bodies of Richmond and his cohorts.

I don't know how long I sat there. Seemed like forever. There was blood everywhere. And it was on me too. And on Ruben. And Erika. They just stared straight ahead as well, as bewildered as I was. It was almost impossible to figure out what happened. And it seemed like I spent a hundred years thinking about it.

But then Lubchenko walked forward. He took a knife out of his pocket and cut the ropes that bound my hands and feet. Then he cut Erika's and Ruben's. The whole time we were silent. Confused and totally mute. It was such a puzzle. Could not figure out what had happened.

But after a moment, as I rubbed my wrists where the ropes had been and looked down at Richmond, who was stone dead and glistening with blood, I finally managed to say something.

"What's going on?" I said slowly. "I don't understand."

"We had to do it this way," Lubchenko said.

Again, silence.

Finally, though, Erika spoke. "So this was a setup?" she said.

"He wouldn't give us the virus unless we handed you over. And you never would have pulled it off if you knew what was going to happen. Richmond was too smart. You have too little experience with this kind of thing."

"Did you have to wait until he pulled the gun on me before you started shooting?" I said, now piecing it all together.

"It wasn't loaded."

"You could have shot him as soon as he brought in the smallpox."

"We needed him to be distracted—it's not that easy to pull guns on these sorts of people. Anyway, I wanted you to learn something, Mr. Macalister. You know quite a bit more about life now, I'd say."

And then, finally, at that moment, I felt complete anger. I paused, thought for a moment about what he had just said, and yelled, "You crazy goddamned freak. Is this some kind of game to you? I can't believe you just put us through that. I thought I was going to die."

Now, Lubchenko was not the kind of man you spoke to like this. Even a guy as disobedient as I am knows that. But I had grown up with a man who could be just as intimidating. Anyway, bottom line was that a minute earlier I thought I was dead. So I was in no mood to control myself.

But Lubchenko didn't seem rattled. He just looked at me, paused for a moment, then started speaking again. "You need to put this behind you," he said. "Your father is going to be killed tonight in Brussels. The plans are already in motion. It's too late to call it off, and it's not really even in my power to do so since it's been arranged by Richmond." Lubchenko dipped his hand into his pocket and pulled out a piece of thick, gold-rimmed paper. "Here's an invitation to the event you need to go to," he continued. "It's called the Midnight Ball of Saint Sebastian at the Winter Palace in Brussels. Your father will be there. The event is very well ordered, very precise. They sit down for dinner at ten. Your father will be at the head table. The assassin will have lined up his shot long before they sit down. And at ten, when your father sits, he will be shot and killed."

I looked at the invitation. Clearly it was a big event—the invitation alone looked like it cost a million dollars to print.

"But what am I supposed to do?" I said.

"You can either get rid of the assassin or make sure your father doesn't sit down. My sense is the latter would suit you best." Lubchenko then held up the briefcase that contained the tiny sealed silicone containers with the smallpox virus. "I'm sorry I can't help, but I have to attend to this."

"What are you going to do with that?" Ruben asked.

"I'm going to destroy it. I have some experience with this kind of thing. Or perhaps you three would prefer to do it. Although you'd better be careful. It's not as easy as you think."

This was obviously a joke.

"I think we'll let you handle it," I said.

"Well, then you have to handle your father, if you want to save him, that is. I'm never quite sure with you."

I smiled, but that crack didn't seem very funny.

"By tomorrow, Richmond's associates will know that he's been killed. I'll make sure of that. The assassination will be called off. Your father will be safe then. He just needs to make it through dinner tonight. He can't sit down. If the assassin can't get off his shot at the table, he'll go home to make other arrangements. These men are professionals. They plan very carefully. If circumstances change, they don't improvise. So either get rid of the assassin, or make sure your father doesn't sit. Clear?"

I paused for a moment. It was not at all clear. But I at least had some sense of what I was supposed to do, or supposed to accomplish.

"Can't I just call the police?" I asked.

"No. You need to handle this quietly. No phoned-in bomb threats. No pulled fire alarms. Get your father to safety on your own. Call the police or the bomb squad or make any ruckus at all, and there's a chance they'll catch the assassin and someone will trace all this back to Richmond, and then to you. And things will get back to me as well, which would make me very, very unhappy, which would *also* mean quite a bit of trouble for you. Remember, I'm playing a game with my associates. I'm not that worried about police. I'm worried about the people I deal with day to day, who are quite a bit worse than the police. This is important, Evan." Lubchenko glanced around the room. "And as you can see," he continued, "I'm a fairly serious man. And fairly unforgiving."

He was right about that. He was a serious dude. No question. But all so confusing. Had to do too much. Was too hard to compute. And as the possibilities of the night ahead raced through my mind and I realized we were far from being in the clear, it struck me again that we were surrounded by dead bodies. Dead bodies and blood. Richmond, dead in front of me and covered in blood. It was quite a sight. But again, we didn't have much time to wait around.

"We better get going," I finally said.

"You'd better get going," Lubchenko agreed, holding out his hand to me. "Until we meet again."

I shook Lubchenko's hand. Ruben and Erika did the same.

And then Lubchenko offered us a small warning. "You might perhaps think that you should tell someone about all this when you get home," he said. "I know it's a lot to witness—for young American teenagers. But you have to let me handle this. Richmond's death will look like a failed carjacking. And I'll dispose of any evidence that might suggest otherwise. I'll handle the cover-up of the others' deaths too. Remember that Richmond was willing to destroy a big part of humanity today, so there's no need to feel pity or wonder whether all this was just. It was."

Lubchenko paused. I wasn't sure if he was done. He wasn't. He then gave us a very serious look and said, "And you'll remember that I can be a ruthless man myself when my interests are in jeopardy. We're on the same side. But if it looks like you're going to talk, my people will find you and eliminate you before your story even begins. You well know that I have resources to make that happen."

Another pause.

"Now, you'd better hurry."

We were all a little dumbstruck. But the discussion was over. And in the next instant we were stepping over the dead bodies and heading out the door.

A fter the door closed behind us, we walked down the hall in total silence. Only Ruben managed to mutter a few things—most along the lines of, "That was all really something."

We stopped for a moment to clean off some of the blood on us. Ruben took off his top shirt—he had a T-shirt underneath—and we used it to wipe off a lot of the blood. There were still spots. But nothing that was going to be noticed. Still, we did it all in silence. Only Ruben muttered, "That was really something," again.

And on the elevator down, we were silent as well, although the haze was starting to lift a little bit. There were people in the elevator, so we couldn't really talk. Not polite elevator conversation. Couldn't exactly say, "I had no idea what it was like to see so many people get shot at one time." Might raise a few suspicions.

And then through the lobby—past the efficient bellhops and the diligent manager and the conservatively dressed employees who were working the desk. I mean, it was quite a thing to walk by these people going about their everyday business, given what we had just seen.

And then we went outside, to the long horseshoe driveway

that passed by the hotel's entrance, and politely asked a man in an enormous overcoat if he'd call us a cab. Again, truly bizarre. We just saw six men get shot to death, and we were behaving as though nothing had happened. We were all racing with adrenaline and ready to go—the mission to save my dad was definitely the number one thing on *my* mind, at least—but somehow it seemed like we should each be curled up in the corner of a dark room quietly weeping, not hailing cabs. But what were we supposed to do?

Anyway, a cab came in about two minutes, and we jumped in and headed toward the airport. And finally, for the first time, with the divider shut between the cabdriver and us, the silence broke.

"I can't believe what just happened," Ruben said.

"I don't think it's going to wear off for a while," Erika replied.

And for the entire cab ride this was about all we talked about. Over and over. Only a few practical matters were discussed. Like the importance of keeping our mouths shut, for instance.

"I'm not saying anything," Ruben said. "I mean, Lubchenko was right. Richmond had it coming. He tried to kill you, Evan."

I paused for a moment and thought about this. But what could I say about it? It was just too heavy to think about. Finally I just said, "I hope Lubchenko really knows what to do with the virus."

"Better him than us," Erika said. "And we couldn't just throw it in the hotel garbage can. It has to be killed properly, otherwise who knows what would happen?"

"I guess you're right," I said. "I think the less we touch the better."

And Erika was right. What else were we going to do with it? Lubchenko would know what to do. He'd destroy it. There was no way we could handle something like that. No way. And frankly, that was kind of a relief. Out of our hands. Our only problem now was saving my dad. Quite a problem.

M ake it to Brussels that night or my dad died.
An enormous task. Again, this is the prob-
lem with dashing off to save someone's life. You
never have time to think about what's going on
around you. I mean, just hearing what Richmond
said to me, or watching him get his head blown
off, would justify a monthlong trip to the bughouse.
Or at least an afternoon in the park. But we were on a tight
deadline. Had to keep moving.

Erika manned the phone in the cab and booked us flights
on the go. Luckily we had all had our wallets with us when
we were escorted out of the hotel in Saint-Tropez, so we had
some resources available to us. And getting the tickets was a
bit easier than getting to Saint-Tropez since Brussels is kind of
the center of Europe and the headquarters of the European
Union. I didn't exactly know all this, however, when we first
left the hotel in Geneva. "I mean, just where exactly is
Brussels?" I asked. I knew vaguely where it was. But generally, I'm a very ignorant young man. I'm not really into things
like "details" or "information."

Anyway, Erika screamed the following: "Where is Brussels?
Is that what you just asked? Your dad goes there all the time."

"That's why I don't know. Why would I worry about a place my dad goes?"

"You're insane," she said, but now kind of resisting a smile.

Then there was a pause. Like, she wasn't even going to respond to me.

"Well, where is it?" I finally said.

"North, Evan. North of here. It's in Belgium. That's a country. In Europe. We're in Europe. Right now. Brussels is where the European Union is run from. It's where NATO is. And I know you already know that because you've talked about NATO."

I kind of wanted to make another remark, but I thought better of it. Pretty rare for me. The fact was that we did have to get serious. We had to plan. And as we continued to the airport, we talked about what was next.

"Are we just going to barge into the party and find your dad?" Ruben asked.

"Yes," I replied.

"What are we going to say to him?"

"We'll come up with something."

"We can't just tell him he's going to be shot," Ruben said, now in a slightly more emphatic tone. "We'll have to explain how we know, and he'll find out that we stole office equipment, and that we sat on evidence that kept him in jail, and that we just watched his business partner get shot. And then we'll go to jail. I mean, tell the truth and we're dead."

"Just trust me, Ruben."

"I don't trust you, Evan. Not at all. You're the least trustworthy person I've ever known."

"I've spent a lifetime manipulating this man. I'll think of something."

"Well, I'm going to be hiding in the bathroom because your father freaks me the hell out and I don't want to be around when he starts screaming."

"Okay. You cover the bathroom. I'll talk to the old man."

"Good."

"Good."

"Good."

43

S o, the airport in Brussels was a breeze to get through. Flying within Europe (even though Switzerland wasn't a part of the "European Union") meant that customs and passport control were pretty lax. Was more like flying from Dallas to LA than flying from Seattle to Paris. And they speak French in Brussels, even though (again, and if you really want to get completely technical about things) Belgium is a different country than France.

"That was the easiest flight we've taken so far," Ruben said as we walked out the huge glass doors at the front of the airport.

"Too bad we couldn't enjoy it," I replied, holding up my hand for a cab. A cab pulled up immediately, and in the next instant we were headed to the center of town.

It was an easy trip, and we arrived at the Winter Palace at about nine. Plenty of time. We had until ten. Still, the whole thing was a very tall order. Just getting in was going to be hard. One look at the gigantic Winter Palace and the high-toned crowd and we definitely didn't belong. Everyone was wearing tuxedos and ball gowns and mingling beneath enormous chandeliers and stone columns.

And then there was the other problem: namely, after getting in, what then? It was not looking pretty.

Still, the fact is that I had begun to have the inkling of a plan.

We quickly walked up the long line of marble steps and approached these enormous bronze doors where a long line of bouncers (big bouncers) sat next to several computer terminals.

I gave my invitation to one of the dudes working the computers and Erika added in French, "This is for all three of us."

The man looked at us very suspiciously and then said, in English, "May I have your names?"

"Macalister," I said. "We're the Macalister party." (If he was going to have any of our names, it was going to be Macalister.)

"Spell it, please," he said.

I spelled it.

In another second he said, "I have only one for Macalister, and I'm showing that he's already arrived. Are you sure you're supposed to be here? You don't exactly look like you're dressed for the occasion. In fact, I wouldn't even let you in if there were three spots left for the Macalister party. I'm afraid I have strict orders to enforce the dress code. This is black tie. As you can see." He motioned to the crowd ahead of us. It was a good point. Everyone looked pretty nice. All the same, it was not good news. We needed to get in. I stood there thinking about what was next but finally decided we should move away from the entrance at this point—we were already standing out way too much.

"Thank you very much," I said to the man as I turned back to the stairs, although this was fairly ridiculous since he had done nothing but hinder us. But he wasn't even looking at me when I said it. Had already started talking to the next people in line.

"That was no good," Ruben said as we walked back down the steps. "But I guess we couldn't have expected much more. Three kids in jeans. We can't get into an event like this."

"So how are we going to get in?" Erika said.

Tough question. But I had something of an idea. There were a lot of people in that building, and there was a big dinner, so I was pretty sure that the service entrance would be mayhem about this time—dinner was an hour away. And in fact, from the front of the building, I could already make out where some of the action was.

"Follow me," I said, heading off to the right. We also drifted back a little so we didn't look too conspicuous. And then I made a proposal.

"I'm going in the back," I said. "But you guys stay here. It's better if just one of us goes—three kids sneaking around is easier to spot than one. If you see me come out with my father, don't show yourselves. It means I saved him and everything's cool. You guys being here will involve too much explaining. Fly home yourselves. I'll get home on my own—with him. Got it?"

Ruben and Erika looked at each other, unsure of what to say.

"What are you going to do?" Ruben finally asked.

"I'm going to threaten to shame my father into leaving," I replied. "A threatened tantrum. I think it will work. But if it doesn't, I'll tell him the truth. I don't have any other ideas."

Pause. They both looked extremely doubtful (as they should have), but they didn't have any alternative proposals. "What kind of tantrum?" Ruben finally said.

"Don't worry about it," I replied.

Then Erika said, "But I'm worried about you going in alone."

"I'll be fine," I said. "Keep the cell phone. If I get into trouble, I'll try to contact you. Stand close to the front steps so I know where you are. But again, if you see me walk out with my father, everything is cool. Go back to Paris and get on the plane yourselves. I'll fly from here. Okay?"

Again, they paused. I don't think they thought any of this sounded good, but we were out of time, and there wasn't much else to do. I was right. I had a better chance sneaking in alone than with two accomplices.

"Okay, okay," Erika finally said.

Ruben said "okay" as well.

And with that, I walked around to the side service entrance and looked for a way in.

J ust to give you a better sense of the physical scene, it looked like this: a high iron
fence surrounding a huge and well-maintained
lot used for parking, deliveries, and all the other
crap that needs to go on to keep a big building
running. The lot was full of delivery trucks, and
there were a bunch of chefs standing in a spot-
light that shone down over a huge kind of movable iron fireplace where they were roasting a bunch of whole pigs. Pretty
freaky looking, to be honest, but I guess it had something to do
with celebrating Saint Sebastian. Maybe he was the patron saint
of pork lovers. Anyway, the big iron fence had a gate that was
wide open, and workers, little delivery vans, and even golf carts
were whipping in and out. The security guards sat by a series of
doorways into the building, which (I would soon discover) led
to the kitchen.

Anyway, I walked through the gate without having to say
anything to anyone and then made it down into the lot, where I
stopped behind a van to watch the two security guards as they
looked over the scene. I'd say I was about thirty-five feet away
from the back entrance at this point.

So, the guards were definitely keeping an eye on things.

But they weren't that uptight. Not like out front. Again, the guards at this event seemed more interested in stopping party crashers than catching assassins. Shows what they knew. Anyway, like I said, the guards were positioned by a series of large doors, several of which were wide open. Seemed like I could take a shot at walking right in—they didn't seem like the most alert human beings on the planet. And I also figured that if they tried to stop me, I could just make a break for it before they got off their stools to come find me. Still, this didn't seem like such a good idea. Everyone down there was dressed in white chef uniforms. They'd spot me a mile away. But then I saw something that might help. A van in the lot marked Laundry. Actually, I figured it was marked Linens (I don't know what the French said) since there were pictures of uniforms and tablecloths and a laundry machine. (I have a very precise and deductive mind.)

I popped open the back, and in about two seconds I found a big sack of chef's uniforms. There was one slight problem, though. They were all extra large. And let me just say that "extra large" for people who spend their lives around food means really extra large. I mean, these uniforms were big. But what choice did I have? I slipped the white cotton pants and chef's jacket over my clothes. Pretty easy to do that. But I looked like I was wearing some kind of oversized Roman toga. Like I had a huge bedspread wrapped around me. I mean, I looked ridiculous. But it was all they had. Had to go with it. Kind of made me nervous, though. I mean, those security guys probably had some sense of who was coming and going. I was a stranger. I was dressed like a lunatic—albeit a lunatic chef—and I was obviously quite a bit younger than everyone. Still, it was now about nine twenty. Time was getting short.

I took a step forward, away from the van, trying to psych myself up. *Just walk in like you're supposed to be here*, I thought, rushing forward like I was in a hurry. Still, I was nervous.

And then I caught a break.

So, some of the pigs were done, and they were taking them off the spit, and one of the things these golf carts were doing was driving these enormous pigs from the huge iron fireplace into the building. Two of the entrance doors into the building opened together, and there was a little ramp that you could drive up. I had seen one cart do this, and as I was walking forward, another was making its way to the door, with a huge pig loaded on back.

But the cart was going too fast, and it didn't hit the ramp right, and in the next second, the cart was on its side and the four-hundred-pound roasted pig on the back was lying on the asphalt. The guards got up to help turn the cart over (amid all sorts of screaming and furious chefs), and the following instant I walked quickly through the door. If I hadn't been in a white uniform, they might have caught me. They were still keeping an eye on things. But I was just kind of a white blur in the corner of their eye when I went in, and white was the color of safety in that setting.

And then I was in the kitchen.

So, the kitchens in places like this are pretty amazing. I could actually spend a lot of time goofing around in a place like that. Long knives, big vats of butter, fifty-pound sacks of sugar. Big sides of bacon hanging from hooks. Pretty cool. Everything a man like me needs to get by in the world.

But kitchens like this are also madhouses—something I can do without. Like, there were easily eight million guys in white running around screaming at one another. Have to say that I also looked pretty out of place with my oversize outfit and my far-too-young face. But these dudes were busy. Dinner was set to be served in less than an hour, so everybody was focusing on their own particular job—and panicking. I bet I could have lit myself on fire and not a single person would have looked up from their duck livers and caramelized turnips.

But I didn't light myself on fire. Good thinking. I simply picked up a large aluminum ladle, poked my head into a pot of steaming chicken broth, shouted, "Allons-y, allons-y, courage!" several times (means, "Let's go, let's go, courage!"—French I once learned at a hockey game with Canadians), and then headed out into the party.

The so-called Midnight Ball of Saint Sebastian **45**
was quite an affair. It all took place in the
Winter Palace's main ballroom—a room the size
of a hockey arena with murals on the walls, a
ceiling three stories high, gold trim everywhere,
and huge chandeliers lighting the place. There
was a giant dance floor, with a ten-piece band
playing waltz-like music. There were bars every ten feet with
ice sculptures and champagne. And (as was clear from the line
at the front) lots of rich and beautiful people. The sort of scene I
was meant for. I did feel kind of foolish walking around in an
oversize chef's outfit. What I really wanted was a tuxedo and a
reasonable explanation for why I was there. But sadly, this was
not to be. Anyway, I had business to attend to. Had to find my
dad before he took a bullet in the head.

This, however, was harder than you might think.

This place was big. Hundreds of people were there. And
there were a bunch of side rooms and staircases and people
flowing in and out from every direction. And a million people
were gathered in these huge clumps, talking closely and
keeping their heads down. I mean, people were dancing too.
But there's no way my father was dancing. The worst thing,

though, was that everyone looked alike. It's pretty hard to tell old guys apart, even if one of them is your father. I guess I could rule out the women. That narrowed things down. Still, there were a lot of stuffy men with white hair, all wearing the same black tuxedos.

But I had a little time. So I didn't panic. At first. But after about ten minutes (now about nine thirty), I was starting to sweat it. I knew my father was going to sit at the head table, so I could stake that out. But best not to let the assassin get any kind of look at him at all. Still, no luck. And by about nine forty, I was sweating it even more. There was an enormous golden clock that hung on one of the ballroom walls, and it was really freaking me out. Minutes were ticking, and I wasn't getting anywhere. Typical of my father. A big party and he was probably having quiet business discussions in some back office. Maybe I wouldn't even find him. What I did not want was for him to suddenly appear in a crowd of people at nine fifty-nine and take his seat. Then things were going to get ugly. Either he was going to get shot or I was going to dive in front of the bullet. Neither option seemed very appealing. And then there was the third problem: what was I going to say to him? Like I said, I did have a glimmer of an idea. Still, didn't know how he'd take it.

Finally, at nine forty-five, I had some luck. Across the enormous ballroom, standing with a bunch of other old guys, there he was, all dressed up, looking very formal and very serious. I quickly started to make my way over there. But then he suddenly turned and walked away. In the next second, he was lost in the crowd again. I started moving faster. But I couldn't spot him again. I now had less than fifteen minutes.

I have to say I was getting a lot of looks at this point. A young guy in a chef's suit that's way too big dashing through the crowd was a little suspicious. I don't think anyone imagined I was involved in the transfer of biological weapons. Worse (in their eyes, I imagine), I think they just thought I was a chef who'd had too much wine. Nothing worse than a disruptive servant. The thing with polite society is that most people are polite. So they're probably not going to say anything. And I didn't look like I had a bomb strapped to my chest. So I was kind of safe, more or less. Still, I was pressing my luck, darting in and out of crowds of people, looking for my father. But I was getting nervous. I was running out of time.

By about nine forty-seven, I was in the spot I last saw my father. But he was still gone. And the group of people that swallowed him up had dispersed. They had sucked up my father and he had disappeared without a trace.

I looked around quickly. But I didn't see him. I looked at the clock. It was now nine forty-eight. Had to make this quick. I took a few steps toward the table. Suddenly disaster struck. A big hand clamped down on my shoulder. I turned and saw two security guards standing behind me, and one of them was the guy who hadn't let me in.

"Time to go, my friend," he said in a sharp French accent that made it sound like he wasn't actually feeling very friendly toward me at all.

"Look, you can't ask me to leave," I quickly said. "This is an emergency."

"Yes, this is why you have to leave," he replied. "It is an emergency to have uninvited people wandering around the palace."

With this, he gripped my shoulder even harder (hurting me quite a bit, I'd like to add) and started to pull me toward the door. And then it hit me. I was going to have to tell all to these guys. If I didn't, my dad would get shot. So this was it. After all my brilliant undercover work, I was finally going to get nailed. I had this very clear image of my father sending me off to military school when he found out all the crap I had done—even though I was really saving his life (I mean, if you really think about it).

And then something else happened.

"Evan?" I heard a voice say.

The voice that has haunted me since childhood.

"Dad?" I said, looking to my left.

"Evan?" he said, again, too absolutely shocked and horrified to get out the next sentence. Finally he got it out. "What the hell are you doing here, you stupid boy?"

"Do you know this boy?" one of the security guys said.

"Hello," I yelled. "I'm almost seventeen, so I'd appreciate it if everyone referred to me as a man. Thank you." Maybe this wasn't the time to be making such a point, but it kind of pissed me off.

"Yes, I know this boy," my dad said. "He's my son. And he'll be leaving momentarily, just as soon as I find out what the hell he's doing here!" The words at the end of this sentence were barely intelligible; they were spoken in this hostile kind of guttural growl that my dad was great at.

The security guy quickly let go of me, but he was still right on my back. I turned to him and said, "I'll leave. I promise. Just let me talk to my father for two minutes."

The guards were motionless and looked at me for a second.

Then I said, "Excuse me, but could we have a little privacy? I'll leave after I tell him what I need to tell him."

Again, they looked a little confused, but they backed up. I was with my father. He looked important. More than that, though, he looked furious. In fact, I'd say that the security guys were now looking at me with what amounted to deep, deep pity.

And it was here, at this moment, in the ballroom of the Winter Palace in Brussels, that I put my still vague plan into motion, the plan to prevent my father from sitting, the tantrum.

But because this is so extremely embarrassing (and revolting), let me just take this opportunity to remind you of one final thing:

Telling my dad the truth was an option, but it was only a last and final option. A very, very undesirable last and final option. If I told him that he was going to be shot, I'd have to explain how I knew because he'd definitely want to know how his bumbling son came across such information. I could make up something. That's true. But if the end result is that your dad's going to be shot, the lie would be just as shocking as the real thing. Anyway, my dad would smell a rat if I lied because he'd want to know every single tiny detail, as would I if someone told me I was about to die.

So, imagine how he'd react to the story I'd tell: that I was consorting with international arms dealers, that I had just about been killed by his business partner, that I had then watched said business partner get shot to death, and all this because last spring I was stealing office equipment from his company and had stolen a laptop that could have gotten him out of jail (where he was because he was accused of a murder he didn't commit) and that I didn't go to the police with because I didn't want to get busted for stealing. Quite a thing to tell the most angry man on planet Earth.

Anyway, I came up with an alternative plan, shameful as it was. "Dad," I said, "Dad, I love you. But I don't feel like you love me. You're cold. You don't care about me. You treat me badly. And I can't take it any longer. Especially now. With all your traveling. You leave me alone like it's just fine that you're not around. I'm tired of it. And we need to talk about it. Tonight. Now. We need to talk about it right now. It can't wait any longer."

Let me say that during these few lines, not a shred of sympathy crossed my father's face. In fact (if this is possible), he just looked more and more pissed as I talked. And when I paused, just after saying, "It can't wait any longer," trying to figure out what to say next, he interrupted and said, "Evan, you're even more of an idiot than I ever imagined. You're going to catch a cab back to my hotel right now, and I'll talk with you about all this idiocy later. If ever. I can't believe you came all the way to Brussels to tell me this crap. Now, they're getting ready to sit for dinner, and I have to go."

They were now wheeling in the roasted pigs, by the way.

"No, Dad. You've got to come with me. Back to the hotel. Now. We need to talk. I need to know you love me. I want to know that I'm more important to you than this dinner."

"More important? What are you talking about? You've done nothing but defy and torment me your whole life. And now you want to talk about love? You're crazy. You're totally crazy. I knew you were crazy. But this is the craziest thing you've ever done. Did you burn down the house? Is that why you're here?"

"Why do you always think the worst of me, Dad?"

"Because you always do the worst. And if you think you don't, just look at yourself. You're dressed like a Belgian chef, wandering around an event you weren't invited to, talking to me about love for the first time in your miserable little life. Since when have you been so moved by such wild emotion?

You're the kid who just a few days ago defaced my car with a broken bottle."

I will say that my father at this point was talking very close to my face—in hushed tones that sounded like shouting to me but that no one else could really hear. And this is what allowed me to tighten the screws, as they say—my father's desperate need for dignity and decorum.

"Dad, if you sit down at your table for dinner, I'll make a scene that no one in Brussels will ever, ever forget. They'll be talking about it on TV tomorrow morning. I've come all this way because this is important to me. We have to talk now. In private. Back at your hotel. About love, Dad. About your love for me. Now. Or I go crazy."

It's a testimony to my excellent acting skills—and more proof that I very likely will be a movie star—that I said all this with a straight face. But I did. And my dad bought it. He tried to resist: "You wouldn't dare," he said.

But this was a bluff I knew he would not call. I mean, just look at my record. I'd humiliated my father millions of times before. What difference would one more time make? And this was Brussels. I didn't know any of these people.

"Dad," I said, "in my life right now, this is most important to me. I need you to come back to the hotel so we can talk. I love you, Dad. And I need to know you love me. And that means more than just saying it. I need to see that I'm more important than all these people."

My dad looked pissed. But a kind of calm and serious look came over his face. Kind of like he was willing to deal with this, but he needed me to listen. He needed me to be serious.

"Look, Evan," he said quietly. "I know we don't always get along. And it bothers me as much as it bothers you. And I'm willing to talk about it. But you need to grow up just a little bit right now. I'm involved in very important negotiations. Very dangerous things are going on in the world right now that I can't tell you about. But I need to meet with several key people at this dinner tonight, and you've got to trust me that it's very important that I remain here. And I don't mean important to my business or my career. I mean important for the whole world. There's something of a crisis afoot, and I absolutely must stay."

And here came a terrible dilemma.

Of course, I was pretty sure that I had an idea of what my father was talking about. And I suddenly wanted to tell him right then and there that I knew what was happening, and that I had even seen Richmond killed that night, and that things were all right because Lubchenko had the virus and was going to destroy it. But I couldn't do it. Funny, but it's not that I didn't want to have that talk with my father. In a deep way, in a way that I can hardly even describe, wanting to have that talk was somehow at the heart of all my feelings toward my father. I suddenly very much wanted to have that talk. Desperately. But in the end, I just didn't trust that he would want to have it with me. It wouldn't be the talk of two men of the world over a glass of brandy where there would be an exchange of stories and ideas based on incomprehensible experiences and a shared heroism. I just honestly believed that all he would do was scream his head off at me and ship me off to Alaska. In fact, I felt that such a real and deep confession would have led to such anger and rejection from him that I'd have psychological problems for the rest of my life.

So I stuck to the plan. It hurt. But I kept going.

"Now, Dad. We have to leave now. Or I'm going to show you how important your love is to me. And you're not going to like it."

Pause. A look of raw anger returned to my father's face. "You wouldn't dare," he said again.

"If you really believe that," I said, "go ahead and sit down. But I think my record speaks for itself."

Again, my father resisted. "You wouldn't dare," he said again. But I could tell by the look in his eyes that I had already won.

"You're not sitting down, Dad," I said. "And since it's almost ten and they're wheeling in the pigs, I think that my tantrum is about to begin."

Again he said, "You would not dare."

Poor guy didn't know when he was beat. But I did. I stepped back, began to unbutton the white chef's top I was wearing, and said, now just above a normal voice, "Dad, why don't you love me?"

And that was it. That was enough. That was all I had to do. In the next second I felt his fingers gripping my elbow and leading me toward the door. "Okay, okay," he said. "But I'll never forgive you for this, Evan. Never."

I think as we passed security, it crossed my dad's mind to get me thrown out and then go sit down. But I was a resourceful young man. My father knew this. He knew I'd find a way back in. So he paused at the door. Looked around. Muttered something that I kind of made out (but would be best not to repeat), and then he led me out the door.

S o I had my dad. And I have to say I was **46** feeling pretty damned cocky about my skills as a delinquent son. I felt bad. Really. I did feel bad that I didn't level with him. But I also felt I had made the right decision.

Still, there's only so long that I can mope about the gulf in our father-son relations. Frankly, I was also thinking about something else. I was thinking that I could now misbehave with moral impunity for the rest of my life. It was my very irreverence and disobedience that had saved my father's life. Final and conclusive proof positive that my years of goofing off were a force for good and not a force for evil.

Anyway, as we walked down the marble stairs outside the Winter Palace, I looked to my left and saw Ruben and Erika off to the side. There were people milling about, so my dad wasn't going to notice them—not if he didn't know what he was looking for.

"I can't believe this," my dad said again, still fuming. "This has to be the stupidest thing you've ever done." He looked away, rubbing his hand through his hair. At this moment, I glanced at Ruben and Erika, who were now looking over at us, smiled, touched my hand to my head, and saw them make discreet waves back. Then my father and I stepped up to the curb.

"You're an idiot, Evan," he said. "An absolute idiot. How did I raise a son like you? It's the single greatest failure of my life."

"I know, Dad. But I'm trying to be a better son. I really am. And that's why I'm here."

"Bullshit," he said (a very unusual swear). "You need to be sent to a psychiatrist. You need to be bullied by a mean-spirited, aggressive therapist who can straighten you out."

My dad put his hand in the air, and a cab pulled up.

"You need to be tied to a post and whipped, and by God, I wish we lived in a society where that was legal. I'd straighten you out soon enough." My dad used the whipping example in cases of extreme anger, although he'd never really raised a hand to me. Says something, given my behavior. What a gentle man he was.

At any rate, in the next minute we were in a cab, quickly speeding back toward the center of town. It was now ten after ten. My dad was safe. And tomorrow, when word got out about Richmond, the hit would be called off. Or so said Lubchenko. But since this leg of my story is now reaching its end, I can tip my hand a bit and say that my father (and I) made it through the night and into the next day with no assassins trying to kill us, at least as far as I know.

Still, the night wasn't over. We still had to have the "talk" I was insisting we have—the whole explanation I gave for my showing up at the Winter Palace in the first place. I can't really describe all that we said that night simply because it makes me want to vomit every time I think about it. I had to stay in character. I had to make the whole thing seem real. But the talk was mercifully short. That's the good thing about people thinking you're a flake. You can change subjects pretty quickly, and no one is surprised.

In fact, about twenty minutes into our discussion about our so-called father-son relations (now in my father's plush hotel room), I decided I was desperately hungry. And fifteen minutes after that, I was happily wolfing down a late night steak as my father lectured me on my "terrible timing" and learning to "behave appropriately."

"You should have waited until I got back. I just don't see why everything has to have such drama with you."

"I needed to get it all off my chest," I said, choking down a big piece of meat. "How are we ever going to resolve our differences if we don't make them a priority?"

Good logic.

But my dad just frowned. "Next time just suck it up and wait till I get home," he said.

I again wanted to tell him he should show a little more gratitude. I saved his life, after all. But I also (and again) decided to keep quiet. Best to let my father continue in ignorance. And my steak was just so delicious that it seemed I was done talking for the night. Time to fill up and go to bed. My father booked me a room on the same floor, and I was in desperate need of leisure and comfort. When you're as lazy and irresponsible as I am, all that activity and planning and running around can be very hard on you. At any rate, by midnight I was fast asleep in a luxurious bed in a five-star hotel in the heart of Europe. Everything I want out of life.

S o the next day, I flew home. Alone. My dad **47** still had business. But he still walked me through the airport (after buying me a ticket) just to make sure I got on the plane.

"I'm not taking any chances," he said. "I'm staying here till they lock the plane's door."

My father did make an attempt to once again address the phony complaints I had leveled against him the previous night. "So are we clear and settled about all that non-sense?" he said.

At first I didn't even know what he was talking about. There had been so much nonsense in my life in the previous few days that my brain had to scan through quite a few details. In fact, at that exact moment, I was really only thinking about what I had seen with Lubchenko and Richmond.

"Huh?" I said.

"Our talk. Last night. The reason you're here."

"Oh, yeah," I said. "Totally clear. I'm so glad I came here to find you. I'm so glad we talked about all this, Dad. I really am."

My dad suddenly looked worried—like I was going to launch into some new heart-to-heart discussion. So I added, "Let's put this behind us. Let us never speak of it again."

My dad looked relieved. But I could tell his sense of duty was forcing him in other directions. "Well, we can talk about whatever you want," he said gruffly. I thought he was going to start choking as he said this.

"No," I replied. "Let us never speak of this again."

I smiled with great sincerity, then turned toward the gates. Airport security was right there, and it seemed like it was time for me to leave. "I'll see you when you get home," I said over my shoulder, almost with a sense of elation at having all this behind us.

"Yes," he replied, looking slightly confused. "See you at home." I think my dad was suddenly puzzled by my light-hearted mood. After all, as far as he knew, I had just flown halfway around the world to denounce him as a bad father. And nothing was really said that could make me this happy. But I couldn't help it. I really was pretty relieved.

F unny, though. As I walked through security **48** and found my way to the plane, my light-hearted mood began to give way a little. No question, I was glad to be alive. And I was glad my father was alive. And I was definitely glad that my father and I were done with all that ridiculous "heart-to-heart talking." But I had seen a lot of stuff the previous day. And I hadn't really dealt with any of it. I mean, it was a heavy thing to see Richmond and his henchmen get shot like that. Psychologically devastating, some might say. And I had known Richmond pretty well. From way back. It was something to see him shot like that. And it was something to see him try to kill me.

And as I took my seat on the plane, I thought again about my family—my father and my mother, that is. I thought about what Richmond had said about diluting the chemo. It was possible. Likely, in fact. And it was also possible that he slept with her. Who knows? Most of my mother's life is a mystery to me—I think that's pretty normal. Who really knows their parents? But it was a painful thought. As far as the romantic liaison goes, I could get over it. She was young. Richmond was a rich doctor. And she clearly made the right choice in the end, if you can call marrying my father a "right choice."

As for him diluting the chemo, I'd say it was deeply disturbing. My mother's cancer was pretty advanced when the doctors caught it. I'm not really sure if anything would have saved her. But a lot of what chemo can do is keep a person alive a little longer and make them suffer less—after the chemo round is over, that is.

But strangely, the thing I thought about most as I sat there on the plane (as we took off, then found a steady altitude) was that it seemed like such a practical, rather than a philosophical, question. I kept thinking about what things my mother might have been around for if she had just lived a little longer—maybe another season of soccer (which I was forced to play), maybe Halloween (by far my favorite holiday when I was a kid), and maybe even one or two more birthdays. It was almost a pleasant thought, and one I rarely allowed myself to have. That is, it was pleasant to think about my mom, to think about the things we could have done together. And I rarely allowed myself to have it because of the sense of loss that always followed.

And this is, in fact, what happened again. I was thinking about my mother—for a while—and I was almost happy doing it, and then the previous two days came rushing back, and I thought about Richmond taking it in the back and I've got to say (and I'll only ever confess this once), it felt good thinking about him getting shot like that. Again, I'll confess this once, and that's all. I may be a screwup, but I don't believe in nurturing things like hatred. And I'm certainly against causing others to suffer too much, no matter what they've done. But I liked it. Richmond was a bad guy. A pretty good test of that was when he pulled the trigger of the gun that was pointed at me. He put the gun to my head and pulled the trigger. He wanted me to die, and, frankly, aside from a few minor incidents with business equipment that belonged to my father, I'm a pretty innocent guy. And Richmond was trafficking smallpox virus. Can't beat that for malice. Killing off millions of people is even worse than killing me, as much as I hate to admit it. Richmond had it coming. And for that brief instant on the plane—and it was just an instant—it made me feel really good to think about what had happened to him.

I guess I can't fully embrace the kind of hatred I was feeling, though. I really do think hatred is the kind of thing you need to overcome, no matter what its origins. You need to think about it, and then you need to resolve it. But that moment, as I thought about my mother dying of cancer and getting diluted chemo, and as I thought about Richmond trying to kill me and half the planet, I really, really liked the idea of him getting what he deserved. Again, it was a kind of sudden and blinding feeling. And then it passed. It really did. And I hope I never feel it again.

And when the feelings weakened, and they brought us dinner, and the movie started, I began to calm down a little. I wasn't fooling myself. I figured I'd have a lot on my mind for the next stretch of time. Still, I relaxed a little. That's what happens when you think hard about things. Sometimes they can drive you even more crazy. But sometimes when you think about things long enough, you can also start to calm down.

But there was one more thing I thought about. It was in the middle of the movie. The earphones weren't working right, and the movie was about some middle-aged woman going off to live in Australia, so the whole thing was a complete waste of my time. And so my mind continued to drift, and it struck me once again that I really did have a kind of tortured relationship with my father. Of course, this was a given. Nothing new about this conclusion. But it did seem strange to me that on an occasion where I really was saving his life, and we really were talking about love, how stiff and fake it all was. But most of all, I wondered if he really did suffer from a kind of deep and painful disappointment in me. I wondered if he really did think of himself as a failure because of who I was.

Whatever. It was all complicated. Too much for a guy like me to think about for too long. Anyway, as I was thinking about my father, I started having trouble opening the package of cookies I got with dinner, and it kind of started taking up a lot of brain space. And as I wrestled with the stupid plastic wrapper, I kind of let myself off the hook with all this stuff about my father and his love by concluding that my father was simply horrified by all young people. It was one of the central facts of his character. So why should I be any different?

Anyway, enough about this. Another thought I had (and a more important one, frankly) was that my dad was still going to be gone for a while and that the first thing I had to do when I got home was throw a big party—to make up for the one I canceled. I had disappointed a lot of eager young partygoers in Seattle, and that's exactly the kind of guilt I absolutely cannot live with.

49

S o, as a further testament to my bravado, I had the party on the very night I got back. With the time differences, it's like you only arrive three hours later in the day. I was on the plane in the late morning and got off in the early after- noon. Plenty of time to put in a few calls to the local socialites. And I have to say that the party was a roaring success—just what you'd imagine from a guy like me. But for as much happy mayhem as there was, the best part of the evening was hanging with Ruben and Erika around the kitchen table (before the other guests showed up) and telling them how I had gotten my father out of the Winter Palace.

"It's amazing the way your mind works," Ruben said. "It's like your brain is hardwired to know exactly how to torture your father."

"I saved his life," I replied. "What you call torture, I call heroism."

And we talked more about all that we had seen—about Richmond and his lackeys and the fact that it's really not a thing that you can even describe—watching someone get killed, no matter what kind of bad dudes they are.

"I'll never forget it," Erika said after we had rehashed the entire scene several times. Then she paused and said, "Don't you think we should tell someone? I mean, I don't want to get into trouble any more than you guys do, but it was all just so much. And I still have questions. Like, who made that anonymous call that started all this off? I just feel like we're supposed to say something. I mean, right now it's not in the hands of any kind of real police force or authority."

It was a good question. But the fact was that it was all really out of our hands. Going to the cops wasn't going to help anything. And we could hardly prove anything at that point anyway. Also, Lubchenko had made it clear what would happen if we said anything, and I was pretty sure his threats were serious. Anyway, threats aside, Lubchenko was handling it all. And I've got to say that I felt pretty confident about his abilities in that regard.

"Lubchenko will deal with it," I said. "He'll know what to do."

"And you're so sure that we can trust Lubchenko?" Erika replied.

I told her I was sure.

"Lubchenko is completely reliable," I said. "I'm positive."

But as the conversation continued, it did kind of hit me that I didn't really know Lubchenko at all. I guess you have to trust some people in life. You can never know everything about another person. And I'll tell you this: I trusted Lubchenko. He just seemed to have a kind of solidity and ethical outlook that made you believe in him. But I'll also tell you this: if we couldn't trust him, if he was a bad dude, he had just pulled off something pretty spectacular—if he was a bad dude, he was now probably the most dangerous man on the planet. He took possession of live strains of smallpox (an incredibly lethal biological weapon), he kept his money (of which there was millions and millions), he killed the guy who could rat him out, and the witnesses (us) walked away thinking he had saved their lives. It was puzzling. And frightening. But I also thought that this was just a kind of paranoia. Lubchenko was solid. I was sure. That's what I told myself, at least. That I was sure. And I was, for whatever me being sure about anything is worth.

Anyway, any lingering doubts I had soon left when the first guests started to arrive. The festivities began, Erika took a seat on my lap (astonishingly, it seemed that she was happier than ever to be with me), Ruben put on music, and soon the party was up to full power. I'm a simple man. When I'm not saving the world, I like to enjoy myself. And the truth is, I really didn't think too much more about the trustworthiness of Lubchenko that night. Fiddling as Rome burned, as they say.

But there is one more part of the story.

A final part.

It came up about a week later, just a day before my dad got home. I was sitting at home, watching TV and doing my homework. I was, after all, in summer school (of which I only missed a few days, surprisingly). Anyway, just as I was cursing the poor quality of teaching at the summer enrichment program—I didn't understand anything about my homework, so what the hell was the teacher getting paid for?—I got a phone call. From France. It was a fairly excited and somewhat upset man from a car rental agency. He was, in fact, calling from the very agency that we rented the car in Champlan from. The car (I now vaguely remembered) that was still in Saint-Tropez.

"I just got a call from the Saint-Tropez police!" he yelled in somewhat bizarre-sounding English. "The car I rented you has been parked illegally for over a week! And now I discover you're back in America!"

I wanted to tell him that it was because of me that he wasn't dying of smallpox at that very minute. This was, in fact, absolutely true, if you really think about it.

But after a little more yelling, I decided it was best if I refrained from fighting him and just apologized and let him continue. "I'm so sorry," I said. "I can't imagine how we forgot it."

This decision to remain calm and placating stemmed, of course, from my deep maturity and ability to remain at ease in stressful situations. But it was also helped by the fact that the screaming man told me that he had Ruben's credit card and that he was going to bill Ruben for what it would cost to send a guy down to Saint-Tropez, get the car out of the police impound lot, and then drive it back up.

"And it's not going to be cheap!" he said.

"I'm very sorry about this," I said again, "and of course we'll pay for everything."

I did feel a bit bad. A bit. But Ruben was loaded, and his parents gave him whatever he needed to pay his credit card, so I didn't feel too bad. Not too bad. And in fact, and this might be shameful to admit, I kind of relished the idea of telling Ruben what he was going to be billed for. And Ruben was the first person I called after I hung up with the car rental guy. Ruben was not happy. But he's a difficult guy. Very emotional. Worries a lot. So I just did my best to calm him down.

"What happened to the fifteen grand we got from pawning your dad's stuff?" he yelled. "Why don't you pay for the car? You must have at least ten thousand dollars left over."

"Well, it's not left over anymore," I said. "I used it to buy back some of the stuff from the pawnshop." This was partially true. I did buy back the Napoleonic sword—seemed like my dad might miss that. But I kept a little for myself. For all my trouble. "Anyway," I said. "Your parents pay for your credit card, so what are you worried about?"

"But they'll want to know what I spent all that money on."

"I'm sure you'll think of something," I replied.

Ruben was upset. But I really didn't feel that bad. Ruben's parents let him do whatever he wanted and paid for everything he did, so nothing would happen—or, at least, nothing like what my father would do if I came to him with a bill like that.

"And anyway," I continued. "You should be more grateful. I've saved your life over and over, my friend."

"You only save my life because you repeatedly endanger it.

You've almost gotten me killed more times than you've saved me. And now I'm going to be in for thousands of bucks on my credit card."

"Ruben, you should really learn to relax."

And this was true. This was something he needed to learn.

Anyway, needless to say, Ruben was not grateful. Despite my ironclad logic. But Ruben is a tough case, and there's only so much you can expect from a guy like that. Unlike me—a man of deep character and many, many talents.

50

At any rate, this brings this leg of the odyssey of Evan Macalister to an end. My dad came home, he screamed at me about my study habits, and avoided talking about what happened at Brussels. I think this is why I didn't get grounded—he didn't want to run the risk of talking about all that crap again.

So things went back to normal. What a relief. But I've got to say that my dad seemed more skittish than ever. Maybe it was work. Maybe it was his delinquent son. It was a puzzle. But not one I could worry too much about. I had to pass summer school or I'd spend the rest of my life at Pencrest. And so, with great diligence, I began my summer struggle for a semester's worth of D's that would somehow lift me out of the terrible hole that I had (yet again) dug for myself.